LONGHORN LAW

Ray Hogan

Wayne Trevison was a man on the run, wanted for murder, when he got the call for help from the old rancher who raised him. Wayne took over the old man's ranch to carry out his dying wish to straighten things out and discover who is rustling all the valuable cattle. But the old man's two sons have their own reasons for making life hard for Trevison and it looks as though only brilliant planning and blazing guns are likely to solve this deadly situation!

Other Large Print books
by
Ray Hogan

Last Gun at Cabresto
The Ghost Raiders
Land of the Strangers

LONGHORN LAW

A Novel
by
Ray Hogan

Curley Publishing, Inc.
South Yarmouth, Ma.

Library of Congress Cataloging-in-Publication Data

Hogan, Ray, 1908–
  Longhorn law / Ray Hogan.
    p. cm.
  1. Large type books. I. Title.
  [PS3558.O3473L6 1991]
  813′.54—dc20
  ISBN 0–7927–0931–4 (lg. print)   90–23908
  ISBN 0–7927–0932–2 (pbk: lg. print)   CIP

Copyright © 1957 by A.A. Wyn, Inc.

Published in Large Print by arrangement with Donald MacCampbell, Inc. in the United States, Canada, the U.K. and British Commonwealth and the rest of the world market.

Distributed in Great Britain, Ireland and the Commonwealth by CHIVERS LIBRARY SERVICES LIMITED, Bath BA1 3HB, England.

Printed in Great Britain

LONGHORN LAW

ONE

Wayne Trevison, grim and silent, stood in the murky, dim shadows of the way station waiting for the hostler to make his team change. The planes of his hard-bitten face were gaunt; toned to the color of winter's dry leaves and his eyes, dark and splintery under their shelf of heavy brows, were but partly open as he watched the shape of the deputy standing near the off-back wheel of the coach.

The late spring wind was cold. It had been cold all day long and the heat from the rumbling sheet-iron stove was a pleasant thing. Behind him the drummer, his only fellow passenger, was having a final whisky at the makeshift bar and telling another of his pointless, rambling stories.

'And then this here sodbuster went and tried to take the wagon . . .'

The hostler was buckling up the final straps. The driver crossed the yard and pushed open the door.

'All right, folks. All aboard.'

The deputy eased around behind the stage, moving deeper into the yard. Trevison's glance sharpened, the man's presence worried

1

him. He studied the lawman's bland face, but it was an implacable face, showing no emotion, revealing nothing of what lay behind it. He hitched up the small carpetbag under his arm. He heard the drummer, speaking hurriedly, 'Never knew what hit him, it was that sudden.'

Trevison stepped into the wind-swept open, small flags of danger waving within him. He crossed the drive in slow, leisurely strides, a tall wide-shouldered man of cool, arrogant carriage. He wore the usual clothing of the country: black boots, levis, wool shirt, canvas jumper and broad stetson hat.

'Come on, come on,' the driver muttered from his seat.

The deputy slid forward. Trevison slowed. The deputy said, 'Hold it, amigo,' in a flat voice and drew his gun.

Trevison halted and wheeled slowly around, allowing the carpetbag to slide lower under his arm. His eyes had become flat, empty; his lips a long slash of gray.

'Well?'

The deputy surveyed him closely. 'You look a bit familiar. I know you?'

Trevison shrugged. 'Doubt it,' he said brusquely.

'You got a name?'

Trevison considered the man in that hard,

disfavoring way of his. 'Crewes. Jim Crewes.'

'From where?'

Trevison stirred. All that way from Miles City. Across Wyoming and Colorado, part of Kansas and the Indian Territory strip. All that distance to this hole of a town in Texas without being stopped. And now, by a deputy sheriff. He considered his chances of coming through if he reached into the carpetbag for his gun. They were slim.

He said, 'Dalhart,' mainly because that was the last town of any size he had been in. And no one knew him there.

'Dalhart, eh?'

The deputy remained still, thinking of that. The drummer was leaning through the window, watching and listening with avid interest, his eyes popped and round. The driver threw a disgusted look at the lawman. 'Hell, Mapes, why didn't you start this sooner? I got a schedule to keep!'

The deputy made no answer. He said to Trevison: 'Just you keep your hands from your sides.'

Holding his pistol in one hand, the deputy explored Trevison's belt for a weapon. Finding none there, he patted the tall man's arm pits for a hideaway gun. Satisfied as to that point, he stepped back. 'Where you headin' for?'

3

Trevison breathed easier. He was glad now his gun had not been on him, that it was in the carpetbag. He had been extremely careful all the way from Dodge City, doing nothing that might draw attention to himself. In towns where guns were worn, he strapped his on; in the few where they were not, he kept his in the carpetbag. Handy but not in sight.

He said, 'Fort Worth.'

'Come on, come on,' the driver grumbled in lifting temper.

The deputy cast an upswinging glance toward him and then came back to Trevison. 'All right, Crewes, get on board. Can't help thinkin' you look familiar, however. You been in Bowie before?'

Trevison said, 'No,' and climbed into the coach.

The deputy slammed the door and stepped back. The drummer grinned brightly, showing his collection of gold. 'Must have been two other fellers, eh, Marshal?'

The lawman favored him with a brief, sour look and spat. 'Yeh, could be.'

The driver shouted at the team and the coach lurched ahead, harness metal jingling from the sudden motion. Trevison settled back in the seat, laying the carpetbag across his knees. Tension was draining slowly from him. He reached into his jumper pocket for

4

tobacco and papers.

'How about a cigar, Mr. Crewes?' the drummer said.

Trevison shook his head. He pulled a slip of paper off the fold and shielding it with a cupped hand, tapped a quantity of dry grains into it; riding easily with the sway of the coach, running full tilt now, beyond the scatter of town. He half smiled. That had been a close one! Evidently the deputy had seen the reward dodger somewhere, the one offering a thousand dollars for him, dead or alive. Luckily, he had not been sure.

The drummer struck a match with his thumbnail, leaned forward and held it for Trevison. 'Give one of these yokels a gun and a badge and they're just a brimmin' with authority,' he observed knowingly.

Trevison nodded and settled back, closing the man out. Outside, the driver's shouts flung back on the sharp breath of the wind. It was colder now and he settled the jumper a little closer about his body. But that was the only concession he made to the discomfort. He was accustomed to it; as are all men who drift restlessly on, never tying down. How many months now? Eighteen – almost nineteen, since that day in Miles City when he had ridden out of town with fresh earth still damp on the sheriff's grave.

5

It was an endless trail. Large towns, small towns, railroad camps, road gangs, ranches; never at any of them for long. The letter had caught up with him at Dodge City, seven weeks after Tom Washburn had written it. Tom had once been foreman for Cass Goodman's Rocking R spread in Montana. He had taken Trevison and his kid brother, both orphans, under his wing and turned them into good cowboys; a substitution of some sort for his two sons back in Texas. Someday, Tom was always saying, he was going to have enough money salted away to go back to Texas, and have his own ranch with his two sons to help run it.

Strangely enough it had come to pass. It took years, but Washburn did leave, and to Wayne Trevison it was like losing his father all over again. But he stayed on at the Rocking R, hearing once or twice from Washburn in the years that followed. And then had come the trouble and he was ever afterwards on the move. Tom Washburn had not known of this when he wrote his letter from a sick bed in Fort Worth. Cass Goodman had placed it in another envelope, sealed it and addressed it to James Crewes, c/o The Dodge House, Dodge City, Kansas, knowing that Trevison turned up there periodically. Trevison had read the letter, near two months old by the time it came to his hands, and started immediately for Texas. Any favor Tom Washburn needed was an obligation that nothing could keep him from fulfilling.

Trevison idly watched the landscape rush by, thinking of that letter. Things had not gone well at the ranch, Tom said in his heavy-handed scrawl. The boys weren't much help, although both were grown men by that time. Rustlers were picking the place clean and they seemed powerless to stop it. The bank was crowding him over his notes, which were long overdue. Could he manage to come down and help an old friend straighten things out? He could take on the foreman's job, long enough to see them through the roundup and the spring trail drive. One good season was all it would take to put Triangle W on its feet. Would he come? And bring the kid brother, too; they could always use an extra rider on the place.

It was no problem to pick up and leave. At the time the letter came he was working on the railroad which had stalled at Dodge City, while eastern money circles floundered in a money panic, that threatened to throttle operations. He had simply sold his horse and boarded the stagecoach. In his pockets he had five gold eagles and a few silver dollars. He owned the clothes he wore, his gun, a battered carpetbag and a saddle and other such gear, now in a gunny sack that was stowed in the boot of the coach.

He realized that traveling would be dangerous. He would get there, do what was necessary to get his old friend's ranch on a paying basis, and then move on. It was never healthy to stay overlong in any one place – bitter experience had taught him that.

The one thing that bothered him most was the fact that Washburn referred to him as Trevison. The old rancher did not know about the trouble in Miles City, and therefore did not understand the danger that lay in the use of his real name. He hoped Tom had not done much talking about his coming down. That could make things much tougher. 'Fort Worth!' the drummer called out, glancing through the window at the gathering houses. 'Sure made that in fast time.'

Trevison stirred his long shape and pushed his hat to the back of his head. It was growing late and a few lights were beginning to appear in windows. They pulled up at the station. The driver came down at once, wiping his gritty mouth and saying, 'Night stop, folks. Hotel inside.' He turned away and struck across the street in a direct line for the saloon.

Trevison waited while the drummer crawled out and then followed. Guns were in evidence on the sidewalk, and he paused long enough to procure his from the carpetbag and strap it on. Inside, he registered for his room, glancing again to the outside where daylight still lingered. The man's natural caution swung him toward the dining room, warning him it was wiser to wait until full dark before making the one call he had in mind.

Ignoring the drummer's frank invitation, he sat down at an empty table and ordered a meal. When it was finished he laid down his dollar and returned to the desk. The clerk, a bald man with weak, watery eyes and spectacles perched far down on a thin nose, met him with questioning look.

'Dr Rogers – where's his place from here?'

The clerk peered at him. 'You sick?'

Trevison said, 'No,' in a curt voice. He waited a moment. 'Well? Where is it?'

'Right down the street,' the man then replied hastily. 'Brown house on your right.'

Trevison nodded and swung through the doorway. Rogers' place was but a short distance. A rusty-looking shingled affair that apparently served in the triple capacity of home, office and hospital. Trevison mounted the creaking porch and rapped on the door.

A voice from the inside said, 'Come on in.'

He entered, finding himself in a large waiting room, once the parlor of the house,

9

he guessed. A small man in a dusty blue suit came to meet him.

'Yes? What's your trouble?'

'You Dr Rogers?'

The man blinked. 'Yes, I'm Rogers. Who are you?'

'Crewes. Looking for a friend of mine. He was here a few weeks ago. Thought he might still be around. Name of Washburn.'

'Washburn? Oh, yes, that rancher from over around Canaan way. He's gone. Been gone for some time.'

'I see. Just how long?'

'About a month I'd say. I wanted him to stay here some longer but he wouldn't listen to it. Bull-headed as they come. Said he had to get back to his ranch.'

That sounded like Tom Washburn. He had a strong way about him once his mind was set.

The physician said, 'He should have stayed. He wasn't in any shape to travel, much less work. He'd been gored. A bad wound it was. But he wouldn't listen to me. Some of those old timers are like that though. Can't tell them a thing. That wound needed tending right close, it being deep like it was. Anything else I can do for you?'

Trevison shook his head. 'No. Just thought he might still be here.'

'He ought to be,' the doctor replied tartly.

10

'You see him, tell him it would be a good idea for him to drop back and let me look at that thing.'

Trevison pivoted on his heel. 'I'll do that,' he said and turned to the street. 'Obliged to you.'

TWO

There was a third passenger for the stage that next morning. A slim girl dressed in a dover gray suit over which she draped a blue velvet cape. Trevison held the door of the hotel open for her, and she passed him with a slight nod of her head. The wind had not lessened during the night hours, and now it whipped along the street in persistent gusts. The drummer was already in the coach settled in the fore seat. Cigar smoke lay trapped in a pungent cloud within the vehicle as the girl hesitated on the step, wrinkling her nose in distaste. From behind her Trevison slanted a glance at the cigar, and then to the man, his meaning plain as spoken words. The drummer grinned weakly, and tucked the weed into the breast pocket of his checked suit.

11

The girl sat down in the back seat and Trevison moved in beside the drummer. The driver shouted his 'Hey-up!' and the stage rolled off down the street. There was a blurring of buildings, of houses, of faces turned toward them; the staccato barking of dogs, the shrill cries of children. Then they reached the outskirts and were rushing westward. The houses gave way to open prairie; with its few trees and the mixed sounds, to the steady rapping of the running horses, and the grating slice of iron-tired wheels cutting through loose sand.

Trevison settled back, tipping his wide hat to the bridge of his nose. He studied the girl from the shelter of its brim. She was pretty, in a regular sort of way and the straight lines of her suit did little toward hiding the interesting contours of her figure. She had, he noticed, cool gray eyes beneath dark brows and her lashes were so long they tipped and curled at the ends. Her hair was a deep chestnut, and it lay around her face in shining folds like a burnished halo.

The kind of woman he would choose if ever he had a choice. But that was not for him. A man on the move constantly had no right to press such a life upon a woman, any woman. She should have things that did not come out of cheap hotel rooms, dirty restaurants and

12

windy railroad camps.

She was wearing one of those small name pins, currently in style, on her lapel. It was of fine gold wire and the script read *Halla*. An odd name, he reflected. The drummer twisted beside him. 'Live around here close?' he asked, leaning forward.

Trevison shifted his attention to the girl's face. She was gazing out the window, her eyes lost in the brown and gray world beyond.

The drummer, not discouraged, tried again. 'Great country! Real estate's sure movin' – movin' right on by, that is!'

The man laughed uproariously. The girl did not turn, evidently preferring the swirling dust and sand to his humor.

'Once knew a feller, travelin' man like myself, that made this country every spring. He got acquainted with a girl in a ratty little honky-tonk . . .'

Trevison saw the girl stiffen slightly, and a slow flush begin to rise in her face. His own thrusting anger began to lift. The damned fool – he should have sense enough to see she was no dance hall chippy!

He said, 'Forget it,' in a harsh voice that brooked no opposition.

The drummer choked on his words and swallowed hard. He turned then to Trevison. In an injured tone, he said, 'Was just tryin' to

13

pass time. Make it a little more pleasant.'

'We'll do without it,' Trevison answered. The drummer got off at Abilene to await the Lordsburg-Tucson coach, then they swung north for Canaan on the last leg of the journey for Trevison. The wind now struck at them from right angles, buffeting the stage with fierce, sporadic blasts that filled the swaying vehicle with sand and spinning clouds of dust.

Trevison reached for the curtain, and finding it gone, shifted and placed his back to the open window; thus shutting it off to some extent. To the girl he said, 'You care to sit over here next to me, maybe I can afford you a bit of shelter from that sand.'

It was placed as a suggestion rather than an invitation, and his tone plainly indicated he cared little whether she accepted or not. But she did, moving across to the empty seat beside him, settling back against the bulk of his body. She made no sound, thanking him only with her eyes.

At this close range he could see a faint spray of freckles across her small nose. Her hands, lying still in her lap, were firm and strong; they were no strangers to work. There was a faint perfume about her, a light sweetness which reminded him of the flowers Mrs Goodman grew around the house in Montana.

The driver's cries were a ceaseless howl in

14

the wind, and the dust grew and fell in varying intensity. As the sun swung lower in its copper arch, the cold increased and bit deeper. The girl shuddered and pushed closer to him.

At once he said, 'I've a blanket with my gear in the boot. If you want it, I'll stop this coach and get it for you.'

She shook her head. 'It's not far now. But thank you just the same.'

It was full dark when they rolled into Canaan, a small cluster of a dozen buildings huddled together along a short, crooked street. Trevison stepped from the coach and held the door for the girl, assisting her down with his free arm. She gave him her brief, serious smile and moved for the hotel, a single-storied structure in which a feeble, yellow light burned above the desk. Canaan, apparently was an overnight stop.

The driver was digging in the back of the stage, and Trevison swung to him to claim his sacked gear. Throwing it over his shoulder he headed for the Longhorn Saloon which, besides the hotel, seemed to be the only place awake. A half dozen saddled horses stood at the tie rail, and when he pushed through the swinging doors, he came to a halt. Dropping his gear in a corner, he let his gaze run the room.

A dozen men were bellied up to the bar. Three poker games were in progress at as many tables, and in the far corner a piano was thumping out a tune under the slack attention of a man wearing a derby hat. Trevison, his throat dry and dusty from the long ride, moved to the bar. The bartender met him with uplifted brows.

'Water. And whisky.'

The bartender poured a glass from a pitcher and slid it to him. He followed this with the liquor. Trevison emptied both glasses. Afterwards, he stood quietly fingering the whisky tumbler, revolving it between thumb and forefinger. The smells and the smoke and the boil of talk moved about him in a never-ending circle. He was having a lonely man's keen enjoyment of them.

The bartender poured another drink. 'On the house. Bad days to be traveling.'

Trevison nodded his thanks, making no other comment. He downed the fiery liquor and reached into his pocket for a coin.

'Come far?' the bartender asked absently.

'Not far today,' Trevison replied flipping the coin onto the counter. The man took it and returned his change. 'Where's Washburn's place from here?'

The man's eyes pulled down. 'You headed there?'

16

Trevison said, 'Could be. Where is it?'

'About fifteen, sixteen miles west of town.'

'Place around here where a man could rent a horse?'

The bartender was looking over Trevison's shoulder, to one of the poker games near the door. The piano began afresh, and a girl began to sing a ballad about a lost cowboy wandering the cold prairie in the dark. Sound was a low din in the shadowy depths of the room. The game near the batwings broke up, the four riders leaving at once.

'Where can I rent a horse?' Trevison repeated.

The bartender said, 'Livery stable at the end of the street. Other side of the hotel.' Trevison nodded and wheeled about. He picked up his gear and moved out onto the porch. For a moment he paused there, feeling the strong beat of the wind, while he located the dim bulk of the stables a hundred yards or more to his left. He debated, briefly, the wisdom of waiting out the night in town and reporting to Washburn in the morning. But he decided against that; it was not late and they could get things talked out that evening. Coming to that decision, he swung off the porch and started up the street.

He heard the scuff of boot heels even above the moaning of the wind. Instinct prompted

17

him to take a swift side step. A blow, directed for the back of his neck, fell short and came down hard upon the sacked gear dragging at his shoulder. A curse ripped through the blackness as flesh and bone thudded into the solid wood and leather. Trevison, knocked off balance by the sudden application of force, dropped the sack and spun away.

A fist caught him high on the arm and he, veteran of a hundred similar experiences, continued to dodge and wheel away. Three, perhaps four, dimly outlined shapes swarmed in upon him. They were coming from the alleyway that separated the Longhorn from its adjoining structure. Trevison fell into a crouch, trying to get at his gun. A shadow closed in, pinning his arm. With the other he struck out, feeling his fist drive into yielding flesh, hearing a grunt of pain. Blows began to hammer at him, coming from all sides.

He braced himself, standing spraddle-legged, striking out with both hands. Time after time he felt his blows reach home, but they seemed to have little effect, and there was no slackening in the punishment he was absorbing. From out of the blackness a blow caught him squarely on the point of the jaw. A great roaring rushed through his head and lights popped before his eyes. He staggered back, hearing faintly a strained voice gasp,

'He's a tough bastard!'

Hands caught at him, pinning his arms back. Fingers clutching at his hair, jerked his head up. Vaguely he could make out the tall, wide shape of a man standing before him, his face half concealed by a bandana.

'Hold him up!' The man's voice was a rasping, harsh command.

Trevison struggled against the hands that pulled him to a stiff, upright stance. Then pain rocketed through him as the big man drove a balled fist into his belly.

Breath gushed from his lips and the night was a swirling pain-filled void through which the wind howled. He fought to breathe, stemming the sickness that the blow had lifted.

'You sure you got the right man?' he gasped.

'We got the right man,' the towering shape before him replied, and again sank his fist into Trevison's middle.

Trevison folded. He hung that way, swimming in a world half-present half-gone. Through glazing eyes he had a close-up view of the tall man's shirt front and vest corners. And the heavy buckle on his belt. In the smoky, filmy depths of his mind, he registered the buckle.

A voice said, 'You got off that stage. Come

mornin', you get back on it. And keep right on movin'. Understand?'

A sharp blow to the chin snapped Trevison's head up. Fingers entwined his hair, held it back and then the tall shadow made a brutal game of slapping him first to one side, then to the other. Starch was running out of his legs, his arms were great, leaden weights. Through a haze of flashing lights he saw a clenched fist coming straight at him. He tried to move away, to escape it, but the hands holding him upright kept him pinned to the spot. It caught him flush on the chin and abruptly it was totally dark.

THREE

Trevison came to with the moaning of the wind, the faint tinkle of a piano and the shouts of laughter – all blending in his ears. He lay still there in the street, dust and sand sifting over him. He was listening for any other noises, any tip-off that the big man with the engraved buckle, and the men who sided him, were still present.

After a full five minutes he concluded he was entirely alone. He sat up slowly. His head throbbed and his sides and shoulders ached dully, and his face was tender to his exploring finger tips. They had made a good job of it. They had really worked him over. He might never know who the others were, but he would know that belt buckle anywhere – and the big man that wore it! He groaned as he got to his feet, the muscles across his chest and stomach complaining mightily at the effort. He felt around in the dark until he located his gun and hat. He dusted himself off, after a fashion, and picked up his sacked gear. He then headed for the hotel, knowing he was now in no condition to show up at Tom Washburn's ranch.

The clerk was sleeping on a cot behind the desk. Trevison rapped sharply on the counter and the man roused. He shuffled up, turned up the wick on a smoky lamp and peered at Trevison.

'Yeh?'

'Room,' Trevison said shortly. 'How much?'

The clerk, getting a better look at Trevison, came more fully awake. He stared hard.

'How much?' Trevison snarled impatiently.

The clerk jumped. 'Two dollars – in advance.'

Trevison tossed the silver coins onto the desk and laid a cold glance on the man.

'What's wrong with you, friend? Never see a man that's been in a fight before?'

He reached out and pulled the register to him. He signed, James Crewes, Dalhart, Texas, in a bold hand and shoved the book at the clerk. 'Which one?'

'Number two,' the man murmured and ducked his head at the hallway to his left.

The room was stuffy. Trevison, ignoring the dust, threw the single window wide and let the wind have its rushing way for a few minutes. He closed it after a time, locking it, as he did the door. Pulling the ragged shade, he struck a match to the lamp and then, standing high and broad shouldered in the center of the small cubicle, he thought back over the fight; considering its implication and possible meaning. Someone did not want him around, that was sure. The big problem was – who? Washburn's sons? Rustlers? The banker? He shrugged. At this stage of the game it would be difficult to tell but whoever it was would show themselves again when they saw he did not leave. He glanced around. The room was bare and plain. Rough planking formed the walls, their intervening cracks stripped by paste and old newspapers. A small circular rug lay on the unpainted floor in front of a sagging, iron bedstead. On the wash stand, scarred by many a boot, stood the usual china bowl and pitcher, and behind these hung a broken, irregularly-shaped piece of mirror, once part of a whole. Large, square-headed nails driven into the west wall supplied pegs for his clothing. He began to undress, stripping to the skin.

After scrubbing himself vigorously with the cold water, he felt much better. The tenderness had become more localized, mostly along his ribs and over his belly. Peering into the dim mirror he saw, with some satisfaction, his face was not too badly marked up. He stretched out on the lumpy mattress, tired and suddenly hungry. But it was too late now to eat. Canaan's only café had been dark. He would have to wait until morning and, thinking of that, he fell asleep.

Daylight pushing against the drawn shade awakened him. The wind had finally blown itself out and he rose, somewhat stiff, but much better for the night's sleep. The same clerk was behind the desk when he came down into the lobby. The man nodded unsmilingly and Trevison deposited his sack of gear saying, 'I'll be back for it.'

It was early but the sun was warm. He stood for a minute in the street enjoying its touch; a tall, muscular, wedge-shaped man with a dark and bitter face. He swung his gaze toward the Longhorn, to the spot where he had been jumped that previous night. He was remembering the actions of the bartender, and he wondered now just how much that man knew about the ambush. It might pay to have a talk with him. But after he had eaten, he decided, and crossed over to the Canaan Café.

He chose a table near the back and sat down. A frowzy woman came from the rear, wiping her hands dry on a soiled apron. He said: 'Breakfast: coffee, steak and potatoes. I'll have the coffee now.'

The woman nodded and returned to the kitchen. She brought him a cup of steaming black liquid, and placed it before him, saying nothing. Trevison drank the coffee steadily, finishing it long before she brought his meal.

Canaan was even less in the day's revealing light. Two or three stores; the Longhorn, the stable at the far end of the street, the café in which he now sat, a barber shop and several such minor places. And then the bank. Trevison viewed the building critically. It was a single-storied structure of frame which had been fronted with red brick. WEST TEXAS STATE BANK, the sign over it read. Tom Washburn had mentioned it in his letter as having a big stake in the success or failure of the Triangle W. He decided he would have a few minutes talk with the banker before he

24

left town. He might even be able to learn a little about the events of the preceding night.

The woman brought his meal and he ate it with the relish of a strong man accustomed to outdoor living. He consumed three cups of the good, strong coffee before he was finished. When he got up to leave, he saw the waitress standing just behind the partition that shut off the kitchen. She was watching him with disturbed, fearful eyes, afraid perhaps he might ask her some question she would find hard to answer. He gave her a hard grin, laid a dollar on the table and left.

He paused outside the door, once again having his enjoyment of the sun's warmness. Few people were abroad. A lone horse stood at the Longhorn's rail, weary and drooping. Further down, a man swept vigorously at the accumulation of sand and dust piled into the corners of his porch by the wind. A nondescript dog sauntered from the stable, and made his way to the general store and there lay down on the step.

Trevison swung into the street and walked to the bank. The door was open and he entered. A short, heavy man with a fringe of gray hair circling his head, rose to meet him. Trevison crossed the small lobby to the counter which separated the customers from the desks and vault.

The banker smilingly offered his hand. 'Gringras,' he said, looking Trevison over carefully. 'Frank Gringras. I imagine you're Trevison.'

Trevison said, 'Possible.'

'Fit Tom's description. Little older, maybe.' Trevison nodded, again wondering how much talking Tom Washburn had done. He said, 'For the time the name is Crewes. Just forget the Trevison.'

Gringras gave him a close look. He shrugged and held open the hinged gate for Trevison to enter the enclosed area. Motioning to a chair, he dropped into his own. 'Just ride in?'

'Last night.'

'You have some trouble?'

'Only a scrap,' Trevison replied. He watched the banker for some sign of surprise, or perhaps guilt. But he detected nothing. Then, 'How's Tom?'

Gringras frowned, his mouth dropping open a little. He said, 'Of course you wouldn't know about it. I'm sorry to tell you this, but Tom's dead. Been dead for near on to a month now.'

'Dead?'

Gringras shook his head. 'He should have stayed with that doctor there in Fort Worth. Got himself gored by a bull but wouldn't take

26

care of it. Came back before the doc wanted him to and the next thing you know, gangrene had set in.'

The shock of this information traveled through Trevison. Washburn was dead. He had arrived too late. That changed matters considerably, throwing an entirely different light on matters; Tom was beyond the need for his, or anyone else's help now.

He said, 'That's the way the chips fall sometimes. Sorry I didn't get here sooner. I would have liked to see him and do what I could for him.'

Gringras knitted a frown again. 'You don't figure to stay? You're not going ahead with the job?'

'Why?' Trevison asked coolly. 'I came to help Tom. He's gone and don't need me now. I owe nobody else any favors.'

'Maybe so,' the banker said slowly. 'But remember all the things he started, the matters he wanted your help on are still here. His hopes, I guess you might call them. I would like to see them finished up right.'

'A natural thing,' Trevison observed dryly.

Gringras shook his head. 'Of course, there's my stake in it, too. But I can live through it. Tom was a good friend of mine. I hate to see everything he slaved for go down a rat hole.'

27

'What's wrong with those boys of his? They're old enough to take over.'

Gringras snorted. 'Doubt if either of them will ever be old enough for that. Virgil's twenty-two, and all he thinks about is that woman he married and acting like a big time rancher. And that woman! Married her up in Dodge City, and she's got him so confounded balled-up he can't think of anything but her! She's a real good looking girl and Virgil is so jealous of her he's bound to shoot up any man that looks at her twice.'

'What about the other one?'

'Troy? Wilder'n a swamp rabbit! Never done an honest day's work in his life. Thinks only of gambling and helling around. Not worth the powder it would take to lift his hat. Neither of them are, for that matter. Both of them were a great disappointment to Tom.'

Trevison was watching the banker closely, seeing the heat rise in him and color his neck and face. He felt very strongly about it, there was no doubt of that. It was hard to believe Tom Washburn's sons could be that way. Tom was so solid and dependable. For him to have a pair of mavericks like Frank Gringras had described, did not seem right.

But then, he remembered, Tom was apart from them for the greater part of their growing-up years. They had lived, along with Tom's wife, with an uncle or some such relative down near Austin. It was an ironic thing, Tom saving and working all that time to build something for himself and his sons, and then having it all turn out as it had.

He said, asking the question for no particular reason. 'What kind of shape's Tom's ranch in?'

'Good and bad. Unless somebody steps in and takes it over with an iron hand, those boys will run it into the ground fast. Them and the rustlers.'

'Rustlers not hard to stop,' Trevison commented.

'First you got to want to.'

Trevison considered that strange statement, trying to ferret out its meaning. Abruptly he shrugged it off. It was now no concern of his – why waste any time thinking about it? He had come nearly five hundred miles to help a friend, and now that friend was dead and needed no help. He could move on, a smart thing he should do anyway, before some over-zealous lawman, like the deputy in Bowie, got bright ideas.

'Still don't figure it any affair of mine now,' he said, rising to his feet. 'My sticking around would do Tom no good.'

Gringras said, 'Just a minute. I got a letter here for you. Probably should have given it

29

to you sooner.' He turned to the vault and from its interior of pigeon holes and drawers, procured a long envelope. He handed it to Trevison and settled back into his chair.

Trevison ripped the flap. There were two separate sheets with a letter of several pages. He glanced at the signature at the bottom: Tom Washburn. 'Dear Wayne: I figured you'd show up sooner or later. Looks now like I've got me some misery I won't be around to tell about. Like I said in my other letter, I'm needing your help bad at my ranch. Somehow I can't seem to stop what all's going on, or even put my finger on it. And the boys aren't much help. They're good boys but they don't have the knack of it.

'Now if you could take over the foreman's job and run things for a spell, I know you could straighten it all out. Do something about that danged rustling and get me 2500 steers to Dodge for shipping this summer and you'd have it licked. There's plenty of beef there on my range. All you need to do is get it together and you'll be all right.

'I won't be trying to tell you who to trust and who to look out for, because I know you'll be doing your own choosings. But you better keep an eye on everybody. I've been fooled myself pretty bad. I hope it won't make any difference, my not being there to work with you. I'd like to have the ranch straightened out anyway and my obligation to Frank Gringras taken care of. He's been a good friend and he went way out on a limb for me. I don't want to let him down.

'And maybe there's something you can do about my boys. They're not bad, maybe a bit wild and hare-brained but not bad. Maybe you can just sort of straighten them out too as you go along and make something out of them.

'We had good times in Montana, Wayne, and I used to think about them a lot. Sure wish I was there to hash them around with you but I guess it's not in the cards for me.

'Keep that fast gun of yours handy and do what you can for your old friend. So long.

Tom Washburn.'

The signature was genuine. The handwriting in the body of the letter was not. Trevison finished it and for a long minute studied it. Then, 'Who wrote this?'

'I did,' the banker said promptly. 'Tom just never gave up the idea that you would get here. Then when he got bad sick, and knew he wasn't going to make it, he called me out to the ranch, closed the door to his room and gave it to me. I wrote it down just as he said it. Then he signed it.

'Just to make sure it would stick, he made out a will also. Left everything to his two boys, but made me executor with the right to run the place and appoint a foreman until the bank's loan is paid off.'

Trevison nodded. It sounded like Tom, the words he would use, the way he would say them. He unfolded the first sheet of paper. It was a copy of the will, short and simple and just as described. The second sheet was a formal authorization of him to take over the Triangle W as foreman, at a salary of one hundred dollars per month and keep, and operate it as he saw fit. It was signed by Washburn and countersigned by Gringras.

Trevison remained silent, his thoughts on the long letter Washburn had left. He could leave, push on to a new place and keep running. That was the usual pattern. Or he could stay and take over Tom's ranch long enough to get it on its feet, thus fulfilling a dead man's request. After that was done he could move on; hoping it would be before someone got suspicious and did a little checking on him. It was a gamble, but with a small amount of luck he could last out a few months. He folded the papers and thrust them into his inner pocket.

'How much Tom owe you?'

'Near thirty thousand dollars.'

Trevison's hard planed face broke a little with its surprise. 'That's a lot of money.'

Gringras said, 'Like Tom told you, I went out on a limb for him. A big limb. That place of his goes under, so does this bank and a few other places.'

Trevison nodded, his face again a stolid mask. 'Keep my coming here to yourself. And the name is Jim Crewes. Don't forget it.'

Gringras smiled with sudden relief as he realized what Trevison's words meant. He came up from his chair quickly, reaching for Trevison's hand. 'You don't know how good it is to hear you say something like that. Tom will rest easy in his grave now, knowing you've taken a hand in the game.'

The banker paused. Then, 'About this name business. Tom didn't know you'd changed it. He's talked Wayne Trevison around here for the last year. Doubt if there's anybody, especially there at the ranch, who won't guess who you are.'

'Probably right, but just keep saying Crewes anyway.'

He swung about to leave, Gringras trailing him to the doorway. Stopping there the banker shook his hand again and murmured, 'Good luck.'

Trevison nodded his thanks. Good luck – he would need a lot of it, especially if

33

the whole country knew him as Wayne
Trevison.

FOUR

Trevison angled across the empty street to the
hotel and picked up his gear. He continued
on to the stable, the matter of questioning
the bartender out of his thoughts. The
stage had already pulled out and he had
a moment's memory of the girl Halla,
wondering what her final destination had
been. It had been a pleasant thing, that
long ride with her sitting tight against him as
the wind whistled through the coach. Women
were no strangers to Wayne Trevison. He had
the strong, normal instincts of any man, and
the masculine appeal of him usually brought
him more attention than he desired. In most
every town in which he had spent any time,
there had been a woman with whom he had
become acquainted. In Dodge, it was a dance
hall girl named Roxie. In Santa Fe there was
Carmelita, in Denver it was Grace. And there
was a rancher's daughter in Laramie. But he
was always careful to keep a tight rein on his
emotions, never allowing any affair to become

too involved. The hostler, an unkempt man in filthy, stained overalls, came from the gloomy depths of the stable and faced him.

'You wantin' somethin'?'

Trevison said, 'A horse.'

'Buy or rent?'

'Rent.'

The hostler rummaged through his tangled hair with crooked fingers. 'Well now, I don't know about that. I know you?'

'Name's Crewes. I'll be working at the Washburn ranch. Just got in and need a horse to get out there on.'

'Why didn't they send one down for you?' the man asked in a suspicious voice. 'They got plenty of 'em.'

'Forgot it, I figure,' Trevison said calmly. 'Go talk to Frank Gringras at the bank. He'll tell you it's all right.'

'He know you?'

The old impatience began to needle through Trevison. 'You think I'd tell you to go see him if he didn't?'

Trevison's harsh tone brought an injured look to the man's watery eyes. 'Well, we don't rent horses to people we ain't regularly knowin' . . .'

'Talk to Gringras,' Trevison said wearily.

The man shrugged and turned away. He walked the length of the street to the bank,

35

and in a few minutes he was back. He said nothing but disappeared into the stable, returning later with a wiry little buckskin.

Trevison dumped his gear from the gunny sack. He tossed the blanket over the buckskin and swung up his saddle. 'Leave on that halter,' he said to the hostler. 'We'll use it to bring him back.'

The hostler nodded and picked up Trevison's bridle, pulling it on over the makeshift hackamore. 'When you get him back here?'

'Tomorrow. Maybe late today.'

'You want to pay now?'

Trevison said, 'Let it wait. Might even keep him for a month,' and rode out of the stable, leaving a perplexed man staring after him.

He struck due west, following the directions he had obtained. Within a mile he was out of the swale in which the town of Canaan lay, and was riding across a high and level prairie. It reminded him a great deal of the country west of Dalhart, the high plains they called it. He noted, critically, the grass along there was not too good. It had not been a wet spring, he guessed. More wind than rain likely.

He rode steadily onward, the sun at his back. He came finally to a gentle dropping away of the land. This would be Nine Mile

36

Valley. It looked much greener than the plateau, and it extended both north and south as far as he could see. Trees, a deeper green band snaking along the valley's floor, marked a stream's course and the flash of silver in the strong light proved there was ample water within its banks. Almost the entire breadth across he caught the faint, bluish smudge that indicated a ranch. That would be Washburn's Triangle W. Tom had chosen a mighty fine place for his spread.

He approached the ranch from its southwest corner, not following the well-cut wagon tracks that bent away toward the town. A windmill grated in the breeze, making dull clanking sounds in the morning air. Several horses stood in the corral, and as he walked the buckskin quietly into the yard, he saw a half dozen men gathered before the bunkhouse.

Trevison was a dozen yards away when he came to an abrupt, attentive halt. Something about the high, broad shape of one of the riders arrested him. The way he was wearing his hat or carried his shoulders, he didn't know which. But it struck a hard, familiar chord within him; stirring up a vague anger and drawing his eyes down to slits. He urged the buckskin forward, coming in silently. The men had not heard him and paid him no heed

37

until he was almost upon them. They wheeled in surprise and stared. Trevison checked the pony, his face suddenly hard-cornered and bleak.

The big man had turned, a frown on his coarse-featured face. He said, 'What do you want?'

But Trevison did not hear. His eyes were on the heavy, silver buckle the man wore. Wicked, black anger swept through him like a flash flood. He said, 'You,' and launched himself from the saddle in a long dive.

He hit the puncher at waist line and they went down in a threshing heap. Trevison came up, hearing the startled yelp of the others. He stopped them cold with a bitter, warning glance that left them still.

'Keep out of this!'

The big rider was back on his feet, shock and pure amazement still slackening the lines of his face. He dropped into a crouch, long arms out-reaching as he circled Trevison. He had lost his hat in the first violent collision and now his hair hung down in dusty disarray. A thin grin split his lips, a sullen anger began to push through his eyes.

'Get him, Jeff,' a puncher muttered.

As if at a signal, the man rushed in. Trevison met him full on – with a flashing left fist that stalled him. He followed this with a whistling right that cracked when it landed. But Jeff was not hurt bad. The blow had been too high on his head. Trevison moved in quickly, following up the small advantage he had gained. Hammering with both fists he drove the man back, the memory of the attack at the Longhorn fanning his temper.

Jeff did not give ground for long. He hauled up, braced himself and began to counter. For a long minute they stood there like that, toe to toe, slugging it out. The dull, meaty thud of fists was a steady drumming sound in the hushed yard. It was Trevison who, seeing his blows were gaining him little except his own weariness, stepped back and aside. The movement caught Jeff off guard, and he went slightly off balance as his swing missed. Trevison, moving fast, brought a down-sledging blow to his ear and dropped him flat.

A murmur went up from the watching riders. Trevison backed away, shooting another glance at them. If they had any intentions of helping their member, they did not show it.

Jeff came up slowly to his hands and knees, wagging his head. He came unsteadily to his feet, blood trickled from one nostril and from a corner of his mouth. Dust plastered a side of his face, matted his hair and covered the front of his clothing. He pivoted slowly about, the light in his eyes wild, murderous. He lunged suddenly. Trevison had been watching for the move, but he still was a fraction of time late. His punishing right and left landed in rapid succession, but Jeff grabbed and managed to reach his arm and hang on.

Trevison lashed out with his free hand. It struck Jeff hard in the face, just across the eyes. But the swing was short and Trevison had no steam behind it. He wrestled with the man as they reeled about the hard pack in a tight circle – Jeff hanging on as he tried to regain his footing; Trevison beating him savagely about the face and neck. He felt suddenly Jeff's leg behind him, tripping him up. He tried to throw himself to one side, to escape falling, but the rider's weight was now against him, pushing him back. He went down, Jeff falling heavily upon him.

'Now you got him!' a voice yelled.

The big rider, bearing down with everything he had, squirmed around until he was straddling Trevison's body, pinning him fast to the ground. A triumphant look was on his face, the grin was back, much wider. With one hand he knocked aside Trevison's lashing fists. With the other, he sent a blow smashing into the bridge of Trevison's nose.

Pain surged through Trevison in a great

40

wave. He struggled to displace the man's weight, but it was an overwhelming burden, held steady in place by Jeff's bridging legs. He struck out at the rider's face, felt that blow miss and clawed for the man's eyes, his mouth – anything that would offer purchase. His hand skated off Jeff's face, greasy with blood. Another blow, this time to the side of his head, rocked his senses and set the lights to dancing. He fought to keep consciousness, knowing only the worst could await him once he ceased to fight.

Jeff was grinning down at him. 'Maybe a knock on your head would help you lay there still,' he said.

Through the haze Trevison saw him lift his gun, butt foremost, and prepare to bring it down. He sucked in wind deeply and heaved upwards, lifting his hips off the ground. Jeff, impelled by the unexpected movement, dipped forward. In that small moment Trevison doubled his leg and struck out at the man's head. It was low. The boot missed Jeff's head but the spur rowel caught him in the neck, raking a long gash that spurted bright red.

The rider yelled in pain. Trevison felt his muscles relax. With another demand upon his reserve strength, he shoved, and Jeff spilled over and off him. Trevison rolled free and came up at once, drawing for wind in great gasps. His legs were trembling from the efforts of those last moments. Hand near his gun he watched Jeff still sitting there, dabbing at the steady flow of blood in his neck with a dusty handkerchief.

Trevison said, 'Get up! You're not hurt bad. We'll finish this now.'

Jeff glared at him with dull hatred. 'Later. We'll finish it later.'

'There'll be no later. If you work for this outfit, you're through.'

The big puncher got to his feet, holding the cloth to his wound. 'What's this? Who you think you are, mister?'

'You ought to know,' Trevison said evenly. 'You said you did last night.'

Jeff spat. 'A smart man would have taken that advice.'

Trevison said, 'Advice is a thing I don't often take, even from friends. But here's a little advice for you. Get off this ranch and stay off. You're not working for it anymore.'

A voice, reaching over Trevison's shoulder from the yard said, 'Who's not working here? Who's running this place, anyway?'

Without turning Trevison said curtly, 'I am.'

FIVE

'The devil you say!'

Trevison remained where he stood, his gaze close and watchful on the rider, Jeff, and on the others who now ranged about him in a half circle. In a low voice he said, 'Come around front where I can see you, friend, if you've got some talking to do. I don't cotton much to men standing at my back.'

He heard the light scuff of boot heels as the man who spoke moved by him and took up a stand near Jeff. He was young, handsome in a weak sort of way. He wore expensive boots, costly broadcloth breeches and cream colored silk shirt. The broad stetson hat he wore would have set him back no less than fifty dollars. There was a smiling quality about his features, a sort of reckless gaiety that looked out of his blue eyes, and quirked the corners of his mouth. The resemblance was there, hidden somewhere. But it was there. This would be Troy Washburn, Tom's youngest.

Washburn surveyed Trevison, looking him up and down in a swift, encompassing glance. A smile pulled at his lips. 'Guess you must be Trevison.'

43

'I am.'

'You're a little late. The old man's dead. I'm running the ranch now – me and my brother.'

Trevison said, 'No, not quite. Beginning now I'm foreman, range boss, trail boss and manager of Triangle W. Not that I give a hoot about taking the job. But a dying man asked me to do it and because he was a friend of mine, I'll take it on.'

Troy considered this, taking no apparent offense at Trevison's words. After a time he said mildly, 'You're a little high-handed with your methods.'

'The way it will be until the job's done. Once it's over and finished and Tom Washburn's obligations are settled, I'll leave. You can damn well do what you please with it then. Until then, it's my way.'

'Still happens I own this ranch ...' Washburn began, the smile fading a bit. Light anger began to push at his eyes and color his neck and face.

'You'll own it when I'm through,' Trevison said drily. 'Meantime, I'm doing the running of it. You got two choices; pitch in and work, or get out of the way.'

'Just what you figuring to do?'

'Good many things. Straighten out this outfit, mainly. And get two or three thousand steers to market this summer and collect for them.'

'That's all?' Troy Washburn said in a faintly sarcastic tone. He was fighting to maintain some semblance of authority before the crew.

'Don't worry about it,' Trevison murmured and dismissed the conversation by turning to the man called Jeff.

'I want you off this place in fifteen minutes. And the next time you walk up behind me, daylight or dark, you're a dead man.'

The big puncher swung a hasty, questioning look at Troy Washburn. Trevison stopped him cold.

'Don't think that will help you. He's no more than any of the hired hands around here now.'

'Looks to me –' Troy began hotly but Trevison sliced across his words.

'What things look like to you don't matter to me! You let a good man down when you didn't stand by your father, and I'm not forgetting that. He was a man you're not fit to clean boots for! Let's get it straight, Troy, once and for all time; you and that brother of yours can rot in quicksand for all it means to me. I'd not turn a hand to help you.' The yard was hushed, tension lying tight over the small group. One of the horses in the corral blew noisily and stamped. Somewhere down in the trees near the river, a crow called harshly.

Trevison turned his bitter attention to the man called Jeff. 'Your fifteen minutes are near up. Get moving.' He swiveled his glance to the others. 'This goes for all of you. Either you work for me or get off. Now's the time to make up your mind.'

Jeff gave Trevison a seething glare and stomped off toward the corral. There was a moment of indecision among the riders; then three of them shambled off after him. A fourth walked toward the barn. The last, a grizzled old puncher with graying hair and mustache, remained where he stood, his hawklike face calm and pleased.

'What about it?' Trevison demanded.

The rider stirred. 'Why, I reckon I'm stayin'.'

Trevison gave him a brief nod and came back to Troy Washburn. 'Any more committees like that one you sent to meet me last night, and I'll come looking for you, not them.'

Washburn showed surprise. He started to say something, thought better of it and shrugged. Trevison reached into his pocket and withdrew the letter of authority Tom Washburn had left for him. He handed it to Troy saying, 'Here, read this.' Washburn read

46

it and handed it back, making no comment.

Jeff and the others had collected their gear and were pulling out of the yard. They swung by, the big puncher giving Trevison a close, burning glance as he passed. A quarter mile down the road they stopped, coming abreast of a light buggy.

'My brother,' Troy announced. 'We'll see what he has to say about all this.'

'I'll not go over it again,' Trevison stated. 'If he needs to know anything, I'll be in the bunkhouse.'

He wheeled away to the rented buckskin. Taking up the reins, he led him to the barn, issuing orders there to the wrangler for its care. Coming out, he found the old puncher awaiting him.

'Name's Farr. Jay Farr, Mr Trevison. Come on, I'll show you where you can wash up.'

Trevison followed him to a small shed-like building at the rear of the bunkhouse, where there was a pump and a bench, lined with a row of tin washpans. Trevison cleaned up as best he could, removing the dust and blood smears from his face and arms. When he was finished he turned to Farr.

'You a friend of Tom's?'

'Been workin' for him ever since he came back from Montana. He was tellin' me about

47

you. Said he'd sent you a letter and asked you to come down. 'Bout give you up, myself.'

Trevison walked deeper into the yard, away from any possible listeners in the barn. He said, 'What's wrong around here, Jay? Looks like a right good spread to me.'

The old puncher hitched at his levis. 'One of the best in the country. But it's a dang sight easier to say there's nothin' right! The boys don't give a hang about the place, only for what cash they can dig out of it. Just bleed it dry all the time. Jeff Steeg, that ranny you tangled with, was supposed to be foreman but he never did no bossin', leastwise of ranch work. Plays around with Troy and does his fightin' for him – and Virgil's dirty work.'

'Virgil any help around the place?'

'Same as Troy. Worthless.'

'How about the stock?'

'Good shape. Ought to wind up the roundup pretty soon. Looks like they wintered good.'

'Understood from Tom's letter you were having a little rustler trouble.'

Farr scratched at his chin. 'Yep. Mostly piddlin' stuff. Ten, twenty head at a time. Never more than fifty.'

Trevison clucked. 'Still runs into money after a while. Any idea who it is?'

'Got my own idea about some of it,' Farr

said promptly. 'And they's some small, jackleg outfits around us. I figure they just help themselves when they need beef.'

'What's wrong with Steeg? Didn't he try to stop them?'

'Never did. Says it's just somethin' a big outfit like this had to expect.'

'And the Washburns – didn't they worry about it?'

Farr snorted. 'They just left everything to Jeff.' Trevison gave this some thought. There was the possibility Steeg was connected in some way with the rustlers. But it was also possible the foreman ignored it simply because of the Washburn boys' lack of interest in the ranch itself. But what of the time when Tom Washburn was alive? Trevison knew that man well enough to know he would countenance no such neglect of duty.

'Couldn't Tom make Steeg toe the mark when he was here?'

'Jeff wasn't no foreman when Tom run the place,' Farr said, shaking his head. 'He was just one of the crew. Virgil was the one that made him foreman, after his pa got hurt.'

The buggy had pulled into the yard and halted at the rail near the front of the main house. Trevison watched as Troy Washburn met his brother and sister-in-law. All three went immediately inside.

'Figure I ought to tell you about Steeg,' Farr said then. 'He's a bad one. You better keep your eye on him from now on.' He paused, a frown pulling at his weathered features. 'I heard you say somethin' about last night. What happened?'

'Steeg and two or three others jumped me when I came out of the Longhorn. Warned me to keep moving.'

Farr chuckled. 'That figures. Sure never forget the look on Jeff's face when you come sailin' off that saddle after him! You'd thought the devil hisself was on his trail!'

Trevison grinned. 'Had my hands full there for a few minutes.' Thinking again of the Washburns, he said: 'What kind of a man is this Virgil?'

Farr shook his head. 'Virg don't do nothin' at all. Leaves everything up to Troy and Jeff. Got hisself a right pretty woman up in Dodge about a year ago, and keeps hisself busy foolin' around her. Guess he's afraid she'll look twice at another man.'

'Jealous, I hear.'

'Worst I ever saw! Causes him to get a mite rough with her now and then.' The old rider hesitated. 'Reminds me. Where you figurin' to bunk? Up there at the main house like Jeff did?'

Trevison shook his head at once. 'No, not

there. Better out here where I can see what goes on. What's in that shed over there?'

Farr swung his glance to the small frame building standing a short distance from the bunkhouse. 'Nothin' right now. Mrs Washburn used it for doin' her washin' when she was alive. Ain't been used in years.'

'I'll move in there if you'll rustle up a bed and some furniture.'

'Good enough,' Farr said and pivoted toward the barn. 'I'll get one of the boys to help me clean it up and tote in some fixin's.'

'One thing more,' Trevison added, 'How are we set for a crew? We're short Steeg and three others now.'

'We just about got no crew,' Farr stated. 'They had Jeff cut down to save expenses. So's they could have more money for themselves, I reckon.'

'How many men working night guard?'

'Two's all. And they don't do much work. They figure the two of them ain't doin' much good so they just put in their time out there sleepin'.'

'What do you figure we need?'

'To get the herd in shape and drive it to Dodge – about ten more riders.'

'Any punchers around we can hire?'

Farr nodded. 'Always a few boys in town lookin' for work. And if there ain't enough

51

there, we can sure enough find plenty in Abilene.'

'Pass the word along then. Forty dollars and chuck.'

'I'll do that,' Farr said and went on toward the barn.

Trevison remained where he stood, thinking over the information he had obtained. It all jibed with the things he had been told by Frank Gringras, and it was not hard now to understand why Tom Washburn had needed help; why he had feared for the future of Triangle W. With two self-centered and useless sons, a foreman of no consequence, little if any crew, the ranch was fair game for any rider with a long loop.

But that was over now, finished. The easy-come easy-go days for Troy and Virgil, and all others who had taken advantage of things, were gone. Even if he had to resort to the rule of the gun.

SIX

Trevison was sitting on the edge of his bed in the new quarters, feeling some of the bruises along his ribs beginning to throb, when the knock came. He was alone, Jay Farr having already started for town in quest of new riders, and taking back the rented buckskin with him. The day was late, near over.

He called, 'Yes?'

A heavily accented voice said, 'Supper is ready. You come eat with Mister Virgil at the house?'

Trevison considered the invitation. This would be the older Washburn's way of getting acquainted. It was not a pleasant thing to anticipate. But he might as well go.

He said, 'All right. In a minute.'

Some time later he stood at the door of the main house and rapped. A voice bid him enter and he complied, passing through the parlor into a small dining room. Troy Washburn sat at one end of a square table. His brother was at the opposite side. He did not offer his hand, merely ducking his head at an empty chair. And in this simple lack of courtesy Trevison read the shape of things to come.

Trevison sat down, his mood changing from the easy familiarity he had felt with Jay Farr to one of stiff, uncompromising reserve. He had scarcely settled himself when a woman came from an adjoining room. Trevison rose to his feet, shock and surprise tracing swiftly through him. It was Roxie – Roxie Davis of Dodge City.

'My wife, Trevison,' Virgil Washburn said, watching him narrowly.

Trevison nodded, seeing that familiar, provocative smile upon her full lips; the cool recognition in her eyes. She had changed little since he had last seen her in Dodge. Virgil said, 'You've met before?'

Trevison made no reply, leaving it up to the girl. He was remembering the words of Jay Farr and Frank Gringras, and he would say nothing that might cause her trouble.

'A long time ago, dear. In Dodge City,' she answered easily. 'Before I met you.'

Virgil relaxed. Roxie sat down and for the next few minutes they were silent, bending their attention to the meal. It was good food, the best Trevison had tasted in many months. Tender steak, gravy, hot biscuits, fried potatoes that were soft and mealy. And coffee just the way he liked it – strong and black. He had his quick suspicion that Roxie had had something to do with its preparation, it was so like those she once prepared for him in Dodge. When he was finished he sat back, drew a sack of makings from his shirt pocket and spun up a cigarette.

Virgil's eyes were upon him. 'My brother tells me you are taking over the place,' he said coolly, adding, 'whether we like it or not.'

'He's right,' Trevison said briefly.

54

'I suppose you realize I could appeal to the law in this matter? I could get you thrown off.'

'I doubt that,' Trevison drawled.

'Watch out, Virg!' Troy said in mock alarm. 'He's pretty tough. Don't rile him!'

Trevison pushed back from the table, all the patience gone from him. 'I didn't come here to get whipsawed by you two,' he said coldly. 'If you got any business to talk over, I'm listening. But to get things straight, Washburn, I'll tell you just what I told your brother. I'm taking over this ranch long enough to clean up your father's obligations. When that's done, you can do what you please with it.'

'If there's anything left to take back,' Troy said with thick sarcasm.

Virgil watched him with sullen, suspicious eyes. He had a thin nose, and a mouth that was hardly more than a gray line. His hair was a sandy brown, his eyes light blue, like Troy's, only with a piercing, bird-like sharpness to them. Neither of the boys favored Tom to any extent. 'Mind telling me your plans?' Virgil asked then.

Trevison shook his head. 'Prefer not. Something I don't want bandied around at present.'

Washburn flushed hotly. Troy laughed

loudly. 'See? I told you he was a tough one.'

'My cattle you're figuring to sell. I think I've got a right to know what goes on.'

Trevison was blunt. 'You don't have any rights. You threw them away a long time back, when you laid down on the job of helping your father. If you had been any help to him at all I'd not be here today. But you weren't. And it's plain he couldn't trust either of you, so I'll just keep it that way.'

The last of the day's sunlight reached in through the window and flooded the hushed room.

'You seem,' Virgil said then with icy calmness, 'determined to do this thing without us, regardless of whether we agree. You realize how big a job that can be if we take it in mind to buck you?'

Trevison's square jaw settled into a grim line. 'I expect as much from you. And you might make it tough but remember – it's a two-sided game.'

'Real tough, eh?'

'You name it,' Trevison said softly, 'and I'll accommodate you – or Steeg or anybody else you can get to do your fighting for you.'

Again Virgil flushed. Troy laughed. 'Jeff sure didn't do so good, Virg.'

'Shut up, Troy,' Washburn snapped.

Troy laughed once more. 'Just leaving! Anybody wants me, I'll be at the Longhorn Saloon, town of Canaan. So long!'

He got up, crossed the room and went into the parlor. Moments later he slammed out the front door, angled across the hard pack to the corral. Trevison saw him swing up to his saddle and ride away.

Trevison, weary of the talk, rose to his feet. 'I'm obliged for the dinner,' he said, and moved for the door.

Virgil lifted his hand to stay him. 'Before you go, Trevison, I'd like to see this letter of authority Troy was telling me about.'

Trevison fished the letter from his inside pocket. He handed it to Washburn who unfolded it with deliberate care and read it slowly. 'Means absolutely nothing now,' he said and ripped the sheet of paper into shreds.

A thrusting temper flooded through Trevison. He took one step forward, grabbed Washburn by the shirt front and jerked him to his feet. The chair skated back and crashed into the wall, dislodging something that fell to the floor with a loud clatter.

'I should break your face in!' he ground out harshly between clenched teeth. 'Only the fact you're Tom Washburn's kid keeps me from doing it!'

Across the table Roxie had arisen. Her eyes

were spread wide and a bright light sparkled in their depths. The fear that had swept through Virgil Washburn died away. He said, 'Take your hands off me, Trevison.'

Trevison relaxed his grip, allowing the man to slide back into his chair. Without saying more, he wheeled about and left the room. He heard Washburn say to Roxie, 'Troy's right. A hard case if ever I saw one.'

Outside, in the gathering dusk, Trevison let his anger drain. He walked slowly toward the corral, thinking of Virgil Washburn and the things he had said. And he thought of Roxie and of Dodge City. She was a far cry from that now. But she had changed little. It was still there, lying in her eyes; inviting, almost challenging, it seemed. She might be married to Virgil Washburn but that would mean little to her. Hearing the sound of dishes in the long mess shack, he changed his direction toward that point. Entering, he found a half dozen men gathered at the table eating. He poured himself a cup of coffee from the big pot and sat down at one of the vacant places. The Mexican cook came in from the kitchen and cast an inquiring glance at him. 'You want to eat, Mr Trevison?'

He shook his head and the cook slid back through the doorway. He placed his cup back on the table and faced the riders.

58

'My name's Trevison. I'm ramrodding this outfit until we can get a herd to Dodge and shipped. It's going to be a tough job. You can expect plenty of hard work and plenty of trouble along with it. If you want to work, you've got a job. If you don't, be off the place in an hour.'

There was a moment's long silence and then one of the punchers got to his feet. He cleared his throat and swallowed. 'Reckon we done made up our minds, Trevison. We heard about Jeff and his bunch leavin', which suits us to a T. We hired out to this outfit to punch cattle, but there's been dang little of it done around here; leastwise the kind of cowboyin' we figure needs to be. Now, we're all willin' to work, and work hard for a good outfit.'

Trevison nodded. 'I sent Farr into town to hire on some more men. Nobody's going to have to work longer than his share of the time.'

'We ain't mindin' that so much,' another of the riders spoke up. 'It's what goes on around here!'

The man paused, seemingly uncertain in his own mind whether he wanted to pursue the subject or not. Trevison waited, making no comments. If the man knew something he would tell it if he desired.

The rider apparently decided he had said enough. He sat down. The first puncher, still on his feet, grinned and said, 'Reckon you'd like to know who we are since you told us who you was. I'm Jules Bryant. That bushy-headed gent there is Jesse Shelton. And then there's Carl Miner and John Frazer and Dub Erickson. There's two more punchers and the horse wrangler, not here now.'

'Only two men with the herd?'

Bryant nodded. 'Yeh. Chuck Collins and Nemo Wilson.'

'I want four more out there tonight. Anybody want to volunteer?'

He had them immediately. Despite the long day in the saddle, they all were willing to do more. Trevison voiced his thanks adding, 'Soon as Farr rounds up some new men, I'll set up regular shifts for you.'

The riders filed out and Trevison followed. He was suddenly conscious that he was tired, that his muscles ached, that there were several places on his body that throbbed. It had been a long and hard day. But he felt better about things. They all knew where he stood, including the Washburns, and just what he expected of them. What crew he had was willing; whether they were able was something he would reserve judgement on.

He dropped onto the bed, too tired to

remove his clothing. The last thing he heard was the rapid drumming of the night crew pulling out for the range.

SEVEN

The early, pre-dawn hour was cold. A light wind, rushing in from the Texas plains to the north, slipped down the furrow of Nine Miles Valley, touching all things with its chilling finger. It reminded them that spring was late, winter was yet master; and had not fully relinquished entirely its clutch upon the vast, rolling land of grass and cattle.

Trevison shivered as he stood at the bench and performed the morning wash ritual. Yellow light blocked the windows of the dining room and the kitchen where the men were having their breakfasts. A rider, Jesse Shelton, brushed by grousing at the coldness. Another man, hearing this, made his observation: 'And you'll be bellyachin' about the heat, come another thutty days!'

Trevison entered the long room, steamy from the plates of hot food and coffee. There was little conversation at this hour, only the clatter of metal against crockery, and the inhaling sound of coffee being sucked in cautiously. Farr had recruited four new men who were having their first meal at Triangle W expense. He had sent word on to Abilene, he told Trevison, and they could expect a half dozen more punchers before the day was over.

Trevison took a place at the table, helping himself from the big platter. When he had finished he stood up. The clatter decreased as the men paused and lifted their attention to him.

'We'll start today shaping the herd,' he said. 'I'm going to look things over. Meantime, you'll take your orders on the range from Jay Farr.'

There was a low murmur of approval to this announcement. Farr said, 'You want to start driftin' them to the north water hole?'

'It big enough to handle them?'

Farr said, 'Yes. Pretty fair sized pond. And then we got the creek there.'

'That's where to put them,' said Trevison.

Farr drew an old pipe from his pocket and stuffed it with tobacco. 'You not figurin' on bein' around?'

Trevison shook his head. 'Not today. I'm paying the neighbors a call.'

Farr looked up quickly. 'Old man Helland and his boys?'

'If he's a neighbor. Understand there were three or four.'

'Four. Helland's to the west. Noble Greer to the south along with the McMahon ranch. And then there's Pewter Quinn on the east side.'

'Nobody north?'

'Nobody anyways close.'

'Good,' Trevison said. 'Now, starting today I want every man in this outfit wearing a gun. The understanding is going to be with everybody that Triangle W range is shut down tight – closed. Any man found on it, not working for this ranch, stands a good chance of getting a bullet in his hide.'

There was a dead silence following those cold, matter-of-fact words. Rustling was a difficult thing to cope with. A steer now and then was hard to account for, and that was the way many thieves worked. The range was a wide and rolling area filled with a multitude of gullies, draws, swales, canyons and low hills, and at night the herd was especially vulnerable. The only sure defense was reprisal; the fear of being caught, of being shot down while on another man's land; or of being the principal attraction at a lynching party. For the past year there apparently had existed little, if any, fear of consequence. But by sundown that day the old order would have changed, the new taken over.

'By dang!' Jay Farr exclaimed finally. 'Sure looks like we're off and runnin'!'

Jules Bryant wagged his head. 'Too bad old Tom couldn't be here and listen to that. Reckon that's just what he was wantin' all the time.'

Trevison said quietly, 'Tom's who we're doing this for. Remember that.' Turning, he left the room.

A few minutes later in the barn, Farr caught up with him. The old puncher laid a gnarled hand on his arm. 'I know I ain't got no call tellin' you about things like this. Kind of like tellin' your grandma how to pick ducks. But you be a mite careful around them Hellands. There's three of them. The old man, and Willie, the oldest boy. Then there's Orville. He's just a younker. But they're all plumb no good, and tricky as they come. None of them ain't past drillin' a bullet into your back when you ain't lookin'!'

Trevison said, 'Thanks, Jay. I'll watch them. You and the boys get that stock moving.'

He had chosen a deep-chested bay from the corral as his own horse. Now, as he moved out under the breaking day, he had again that feeling of well-being which always filled him when in the saddle. A rider since he could recall, he was never fully at home on the ground. Like all such men, walking was a painful chore. The times when he did jobs on the railroad gangs were sheer misery, since they called for his being on his feet.

Forking a horse was a natural part of him. Loping easily along with the keen slice of the breeze upon him, he had a moment's brief wish that it could always be that way. It would be a fine thing to believe he could spend the rest of his life aboard a fine animal like the bay, covering the range of a good ranch like the Triangle W that was his own.

But it was an empty wish, a lost hope. They would never let him rest. To kill a sheriff was a crime second to none, and every lawman automatically assumed the role of avenger for his fallen clansman. Few people ever stopped to consider that there could be black sheep in that order also; that a lawman could be anything but honorable and true.

It did things to a man. It filled him with an understanding of life's futility, of its temporal quality. It made high-flung ambitions and beautiful dreams of little value, and placed a price of exaggerated importance upon escape and freedom.

The grass was better on this part of the range than he had expected it to be. In the down flooding sunlight that spread swiftly, once released from its imprisoning hills far to the east, it sparkled brightly. And as the chill began to lift, the sweet smell of it lifted and became a perfume in the air.

Trevison rode for a good hour, striking due west. He saw scattered patches of cattle grazing and riding close to such clusters, he found them to be Triangle W stock, all unattended. He paused to think of that, but passed it off after a moment. That would be taken care of now. Farr and the crew would start that day rounding up the stray parts of the scattered herd, collecting them eventually on the north section of the ranch.

He rode on and a few minutes later topped a low ridge and looked down upon a decaying group of buildings. This would be the Helland place. For a time he studied it, noting the gray structure, the sagging corrals, the absence of activity. A half dozen steers were milling about in a small yard near the barn. Three horses dozed at the tie rail. A lopsided wagon, its tongue canted to an odd angle, stood in the center of the hard pack. The whole place had the forlorn appearance of abandonment.

Trevison dropped back below the ridge and followed out its full run, thus coming into Hellands from its extreme western end. He wanted to have first a look at those steers in the pen. He eased up to them from the off-side of the barn, which was little more than a hollow shell. They lifted their heads at his approach. All young, surprisingly fat animals for this time of year. Trevison circled them, suspicion riding him hard. They were unbranded, bearing no marks of any sort and that, in itself, was wrong. He drifted quietly deeper into the yard, narrow eyes prying sharply for hides, or other evidence, that would prove the conclusion he felt certain was true. But he could find no more. Only the empty structures, long unused. One thing certain, whatever it was that kept the Helland bunch alive, it was not ranching.

He rode the bay to the front of the largest shack which seemed to be the housing point. Then, scanning the range at his back, he called out: 'Helland!'

Almost at once the door kicked back and a man stepped out onto the porch. He threw a hard, questioning glance at Trevison and moved on into the yard, a short and heavy man with thick shoulders, bull neck, and flaming red hair which extended down the sides of his face into a matching beard.

'You Helland?'

The old man nodded. 'What do y'want?'

'Give you a little advice. I don't know where those steers in your corral came from but I've got a pretty fair idea.'

67

The door opened again. Two more men came out, younger duplicates of the elder Helland. This would be Willie, wearing a gun on his hip. Orville carried a single-barreled shotgun. Trevison waited while they lined up, one on either side of his father.

'I want advice, I ask for it,' Helland stated in a flat tone.

'Here's some you're getting anyway. Stay off Triangle W range. I'll tell you this time. Any of you caught on it after now is a dead man. That clear?'

The boy with the shotgun stirred angrily. Helland stayed him with a backward sweep of his hand.

'You accusin' me of rustlin'?'

'Take it any way you like. I'm telling you and your pups what you'd better not do!'

Helland said something out of the corner of his mouth to Willie, which Trevison could not hear. In a slightly mocking tone he said, 'Mighty big talk, comin' from the Washburn bunch. You reckon you can back it up?'

Trevison was watching Willie, the Helland with the pistol on his hip. If there was trouble coming, that was where it would spring from. And come it did. Trevison saw the sudden, betraying break in the man's expression in that fragment of time before he clawed for his gun. Trevison, in a single, fluid motion,

68

drew and fired. He laid the bullet at old man Helland's feet, kicking dirt over his boots. The red-headed man yelled and jumped back.

Willie, his gun still holstered, let his hand fall slowly away. Trevison said, 'The next one will be in your belly. But I don't think it will be necessary. Now toss those guns out there into the middle of the yard.'

He waited, watching narrowly, while Willie pulled the heavy pistol and threw it to the indicated spot. Orville did not at once follow suit. Helland muttered something to him and he dropped the shotgun.

'Where's your herd?' Trevison asked unexpectedly.

'What herd?' the old man answered without thinking. Then, with a wave of his hand, 'Oh, I reckon it's over there on the other side of the hill. Drifts around right smart.'

Trevison's laugh was a harsh, grating sound. 'You're a damn poor liar, Helland. You don't have a herd. You're rustling beef, every pound that you get. You're butchering and selling. That's how you're living. Well, think up something else, old man. That's finished now. You'll rustle no more Triangle W stock and live to enjoy it.'

He slid his gun back into its holster and pulled the bay around. 'Any of you interested in dying right now, just make a move for one of those guns before I'm out of sight.'

Keeping half turned in the saddle, he rode slowly from the yard. His last glimpse of the Hellands, before he dropped into a draw, was the coppery shine of sunlight on their flaming hair.

No doubt that was where some of the Washburn beef was going. But in his own mind Trevison knew the quantity was small. Just a few head now and then to keep them in cash. But it all counted up. At fifteen or twenty dollars a head, it graduated into real money. And if Helland was getting away with it, so also must be the others.

He followed out a long valley coming upon a small herd at its termination. They wore an N-G brand, for Noble Greer no doubt. A mile later he spotted the ranch, lying in a semicircle of trees, with the bright slash of a stream cutting across the back of it. Here again he swung wide, approaching the buildings on their blind side. The place was clean, well kept, in sharp contrast to the Helland ranch.

Reaching the barn he heard the steady thud of a blacksmith working at iron. Directly ahead was the calf yard, and in it he saw a bunch of steers. He rode quietly up to the pole fence and threw his sharp glance at the animals. Anger brushed swiftly through him. Every steer in the pen bore the Triangle W brand! Methodically he counted them; twenty-five. Twenty-five head of Washburn stock penned there in brazen, impudent disregard of all who might come and see, awaiting a running iron!

He sawed the bay around and rode straight up to the house, his mouth a hard line. His eyes were glittering fires beneath dark brows and a cold driving anger was rushing through him. He pulled up a dozen feet away from the door.

'Greer! Come out!'

The steady strike of the hammer in the barn ceased. Trevison moved in the saddle, sliding half about to where he could keep his gaze on that building also. The door of the house opened. Trevison's thudding temper focused on that point. He would actually be justified in shooting Greer down where he stood! Or any man who would rustle stock and pen it right in his own yard! He must be dead certain of himself, having absolutely no fear whatever of retaliation!

A figure came through the shadowy square of doorway and stepped off the porch. Trevison stared. A frown broke across his face. It was the girl from the stagecoach, Halla. She met his look with that serious half smile he remembered so well; that he had not been entirely able to erase from his memory.

'Hello. What brings you way out here?'

Trevison, shock stiffening his tongue and making words hard to come by, said, 'This your place?'

'My father's,' she answered. 'I'm Halla Greer.'

EIGHT

The recollection of the Triangle W steers in the corral brought Trevison back to the moment. In a terse voice he said, 'Your father here?'

Halla looked at him closely, aware of the brittle change in his manner and tone. 'Why, yes. He's in the barn.' She swung her glance to that building. A man was coming through the doorway, tossing aside a leather apron as he did so. Apparently it had been Greer himself working at the forge. He crossed the yard leisurely, a thin, slight man with a noticeable limp. When he drew up beside the girl, Trevison saw he had the same gray eyes.

'What is it, Halla?'

She shook her head, frowning slightly. There was some danger here, she sensed;

72

some threat in the big man sitting silently on the bay horse. 'I don't know. He wants to see you.'

Greer turned then to Trevison. 'Something on your mind?'

'Like to know what you're doing with Triangle W stock in your corral?'

'Doing with it?' Greer echoed. 'Why, I'm getting ready to slap my own brand on them! Why? Who are you and what business is it of yours?'

'Name's Trevison. I'm running the Washburn spread and I'm looking for missing stock.'

Halla Greer and her father exchanged looks. He said, 'You're running Triangle W?'

Trevison said, 'I am. Now, what about those steers?'

Greer wagged his head. 'Those are mine. Bought and paid for in hard cash.'

Trevison gave the man a slanting look. 'Bought from who?'

At this inference Greer bristled. 'Since that's a deal that took place some days back, I don't figure it any of your business.'

'I'm making it my business,' Trevison stated in a winter cold voice. 'Either you show me a bill of sale or I'm taking them back with me.'

He was aware of Halla's close gaze. She was

73

watching him with something like distaste in her eyes. Yet there was a trace of fear there, too.

'Could be a fair chore,' Greer said coldly. 'I've got a few men around.'

'Not enough to keep you from getting hurt,' Trevison said brusquely. 'Do I see that bill of sale or not?'

Halla spoke then, the first time since her father had arrived. 'I guess I made a mistake. You're not the same man I was with on the stagecoach,' she observed, with womanly candor. 'Show him the receipt, papa. Then maybe he will move on and leave us alone.'

Greer had turned to her. 'You say this is the man you saw on the stage?'

She nodded. Greer shook his head. 'You must have had a touch of the sun,' he commented and wheeling about, started for the house. 'I'll get that receipt.'

Halla remained in the yard. She was wearing levis and a faded, checked shirt. Lifting her eyes suddenly, she caught Trevison frankly appraising her. She returned his study coolly. After a moment he turned away, a heaviness within him. Odd how some things got into a man, and never let him completely rest; never fully left him. He had tried to forget this Halla Greer ever since they had got off the stage in Canaan. And just when

74

he was making some progress along that line, wrapping himself in a job that was to be done, here she was again, standing before him proud and unyielding as lava rock.

Noble Greer was back in short minutes, holding a slip of paper in his hand. He paused in front of Trevison, uncertain of his trust in the dark-faced man who watched him so narrowly.

Trevison ended that. He said, 'It's safe,' and reaching, plucked it from his fingers.

It was a bill of sale. Made out to Noble Greer for twenty-five steers. Sum, two hundred fifty dollars. It was signed by Troy Washburn.

Trevison handed it back to the rancher, anger once again having its strong way with him. That was Troy's way of keeping himself supplied with cash for his gambling and drinking; rustling his own cattle, actually, and selling them to other ranchers. And the price – ten dollars a head. Barely half their worth.

A hard twist in his voice, he commented, 'A real good buy, Greer. A bargain.'

Greer grimaced. 'Sure, otherwise I wouldn't have bought them. Troy said he needed to raise some quick money and offered them to me. I bought them. Any rancher would have done the same.'

In a tone that left no room for misunderstanding, Trevison said, 'It's a bargain you can forget. We're selling no stock to anybody. I'll send word in to Frank Gringras to give you your money back. Tomorrow I'll have a couple of riders here for the steers.'

'Now wait a minute,' Greer protested. 'I bought those from Troy . . .'

'Makes no difference. It's no deal. And if he ever shows up here again trying to peddle you any Triangle W cattle, leave it alone. I'll be right behind him to take them home. And next time there won't be any refund.'

'You mean Troy's got no authority . . .'

'Troy or Virgil or anybody else around here – but me. And while we're talking about it, Triangle W range is closed. Orders are to shoot anybody found on it. You got any business to transact, use the road and stay on it all the way.'

Halla still watched him with that disturbed, almost repelled air. In a brave voice she said, 'I do believe Mr Trevison is accusing us of rustling.'

Trevison saw no humor in it. He said, 'No, not that. I can't put you in the same wagon with the Hellands. But I want no mistakes made. I don't want to bury anybody that doesn't have it coming.'

76

'No, of course not,' she said. 'You're the kind of man that never does such things.'

Trevison's glance settled upon her as he attempted to fathom her meaning. 'Only when necessary,' he said soberly.

'Killing – when necessary?'

'If necessary,' Trevison replied quietly. He swung his attention back to Noble Greer. 'No hard feelings, I hope. But something like this had to be set straight, once and for all time.'

'Sure, no hard feelings,' the rancher agreed. 'I just never questioned Troy's motives. If a man can't figure on his own future son-in-law, then I don't know who he can figure on.'

Trevison touched the brim of his hat to Halla, nodded to the rancher and wheeled out of the yard. Minutes later Greer's words caught up with his thoughts. Future son-in-law – Halla was planning to marry Troy! It came as a mild shock, and he considered it for some time. Finally he shook his head. Halla Greer was entitled to something better than Troy Washburn. She was a mighty fine woman to be wasted on such as he. She deserved more . . .

McMahon's place was a duplication of Greer's, only years older. The rancher and his wife were not there, Trevison learned after he had made his quiet examination of the premises. A cowboy, aroused from the bunkhouse, said they were in town.

'Back soon?'

'Prob'ly not before dark.'

'You bought any Triangle W stock lately?' Trevison asked then.

The cowboy shook his head. 'Not that I can recollect. Month, maybe two month back.'

'Troy Washburn handle the deal?'

A frown crowded the man's face. 'Say, who the hell are you, anyway? Comin' 'round here askin' questions?'

'Answer the question,' Trevison snapped. 'Was it Troy?'

The rider gave Trevison a startled look. 'I reckon it was. He always did handle it.'

Trevison settled back in his saddle, his face dark and stern. 'You tell McMahon from now on he's not to buy Triangle W stock from anybody. You got that? And tell him, and everybody else around here that Triangle W range is closed. It's a dangerous place to be if you're not working there for them.'

Before the rider could make any reply, Trevison pulled the bay around and loped from the yard.

One more stop. Pewter Quinn. It was some time after midday when he rode out of a draw, and saw the place. Small, no larger than Greer's, but in much worse condition.

Yet there appeared to be considerable activity about the yard and around the buildings. It was not going to be possible to look over the place first, as he had done the others. At least a half dozen riders were in plain sight.

Trevison rode straight in, heading for a corral fence upon which several hides had been draped to dry. While a surprised puncher watched, he probed about the skins until he found what he wanted; the triangle with its center W burned into the hide.

He wheeled to the man. 'Where's Quinn?'

The man ducked his head toward another corral. 'Over there, workin'.'

Trevison walked the bay to that point. A stocky, bare-waisted man wrestled with an untamed buckskin in a square of yard. The horse was fighting the leathers and as Trevison approached, he reared and struck out with his forelegs. The stocky man ducked away, neatly, seeing in that moment, Trevison.

He said, 'What do you want?' in an impatient, demanding sort of way. 'I don't need no riders.'

Trevison was brief. 'Where'd you get those hides hanging on your fence?'

Quinn, sweat streaming down his face and neck and onto his hairy chest, wrapped the reins of the bronco around a snubbing post.

He moved closer to Trevison, placing his hands on his hips. 'What's it to you, mister?'

'Plenty,' Trevison shot back. 'I'm looking for rustled Triangle W stock. Looks like I've found it.'

Quinn's eyes flared. He took a quick step forward, his arms going down.

'Hold it!' Trevison barked. 'And keep your hand away from that gun!'

Quinn halted abruptly. He covered Trevison with an appraising look. A slow smile came to his mouth. 'Just how far you think you'll get pulling that hard case stuff on me? One yell and I'll have a half dozen men on your back.'

'Fine. They can dig the bullets out of your belly,' Trevison said coldly. 'Now show some sense and answer my questions. How did that Triangle W stock get here?'

Pewter Quinn searched Trevison's grim face for a clue to something that was in his mind. Apparently finding it, he shrugged. 'Bought them. How else?'

'Bought them from who?'

'Troy Washburn. Last week.'

Trevison thought for a moment. 'You bought many from him?'

'Whenever he comes along with a good price. That's what I'm in the business for – to make money.'

80

Trevison said, 'That's over with now. Don't buy any more from him, no matter how good the price is.'

Quinn squared himself. 'Reckon that's up to me. I see a bargain, by granny, I'll take it.'

'Not if it's Triangle W stock. You buy any more from him, or anybody else, I'll be here after it. That's a warning, Quinn.'

'You talk a little wide. Think you can back up that kind of talk?'

Trevison smiled. 'Try me and see.'

The threat of the man was a solid force, making its presence felt in the small yard. Pewter Quinn watched silently for a full minute. Then his gaze wavered and fell. 'Well, of course, if he don't make me no offer . . .'

'Offer or not,' Trevison slashed through his words, 'forget it. Don't buy. And there's one more thing for you to remember; Triangle W range is closed. Keep off it and keep your riders off.'

'Who says we're on it?'

'Nobody. I'm just telling you it's closed.'

Quinn shrugged. 'So it's closed. All right. What did you say your name was?'

'I didn't say, but it's Trevison.'

'You take over the Washburn ranch?'

Trevison said, 'Right. Any business you've

got to handle, see me about it.'

'What about Troy and the other boy – Virgil, or whatever his name is?'

'They'll be around, but no more than that. What did you pay Troy for that beef?'

'Ten dollars a head.'

'You didn't buy then, you got them as a gift,' Trevison commented and wheeled about. 'Don't take any more bargains from him, Quinn. It's likely to cost you a lot more than you're ready to pay.'

He did not wait for the rancher's reply but rode from the yard. Ten dollars a head for good beef! The very thought of it angered Trevison. But Troy Washburn had rustled his last beef at Triangle W. He could mark that down for a dead certain fact.

NINE

When Trevison rode into the yard at Washburn's, he was thinking again of Halla Greer and this disturbed him. There was no place in his future for a woman such as she. Affairs of short duration, like that with Roxie Davis, or the senorita in Santa Fe, were all right. They were soon over, forgotten in a

82

few weeks. But Halla Greer was affecting him differently. She was threatening to upset the carefully calculated void of future he had programmed for himself.

It was near supper time and the long ride had built a hunger within him. He rode straight to the corral and released the bay. Farr and two of the new riders were washing up, and the old puncher, finished, waited aside for Trevison to complete his own chore.

When he finished Farr said, 'Well, you meet the neighbors?'

Trevison said, 'All but the McMahons. He wasn't home. I left word with one of his crew.'

'Any trouble?'

'Not specially. Helland's got a pair of anxious boys.'

Farr threw him a quick shrewd glance. 'You have to do anything about that?'

Trevison shrugged. 'Just dusted off the old man's boots. Nobody hurt.'

Jay Farr chuckled. 'Bet that hurt his pride some! He's so all fired proud of Willie, and thinkin' he's such shuckin's with a gun.'

Trevison said, 'I dropped a warning to them all. They know this range is closed and we'll back it up with guns if need be. The crew understand that?'

Farr ducked his head. 'Includin' the new boys in from Abilene. Three of them.'

Trevison pivoted toward his quarters. Abruptly he halted and swiveled his attention back to Farr. 'You know Troy was selling beef to these other ranchers?'

The old puncher plucked at his chin. 'Nope. Not for sure, anyway. Had me an idea or two about it. Jeff and him sort of kept things like that to themselves.'

'Looks like he had a regular market going. Seems every time he needed some cash, he'd run a small jag of cattle down and sell off to one of them.'

'Bill of sale, too?'

Trevison nodded. 'Everything just right. Can't very well blame the ranchers for not picking up a bargain when they found one. But I don't figure they'll be buying any more.'

He turned back for his bunkhouse. Some slight noise from within the small building laid its quick caution upon him as he reached for the knob. He hesitated, old wariness, born of suspicion for every unknown sound and shadow, setting him careful. It came from the endless trails, from never knowing what was around a corner, or who stood on the far side of a closed door. It was a part of the cloth, a piece of the whole pattern which began that day in Miles City.

He drifted to the side, easing away from the door. One hand resting on the gun at his hip, he reached for the knob and threw the door wide.

'Come out!'

There was the immediate sound of a chair scraping against the floor, the dry rustle of corded clothing. And then Troy Washburn stood framed in the doorway.

Trevison relaxed slowly. In a low voice he said, 'Don't ever do that again.'

'Do what?' Washburn asked, his face puzzled.

'Sit in a dark room and wait for me. Next time light the lamp.'

Troy Washburn stared. A slow smile broke across his mouth. 'You afraid of the dark?'

Trevison shook his head. 'Only like to know who's in it.'

Troy regarded him thoughtfully. 'You don't like a man standing behind you – at your back. You don't like somebody to wait for you in the dark. You've got some strange ideas, Trevison.'

'Nothing strange about them,' Trevison said shortly. 'Something on your mind?'

Washburn said, 'Yes, you. I stopped by the Greers' on my way back from town. Understand you were there today, doing a lot of big talking.'

85

'I was there,' Trevison agreed.

'You're a bit out of line, throwing your weight around with people like them. They're close friends of mine.'

'Friends or not, they're buying no more beef from this ranch. You're not selling them, or anybody else, any more Triangle W stock!'

'Anybody else?'

'McMahon – Quinn – Helland. Anybody.'

The mention of Helland's name was a shot in the dark. But it apparently struck true. Trevison waited for Washburn to make a denial but he did not.

Instead, he said, 'I don't appreciate your sneaking around behind my back talking about . . .'

'Makes no difference what you think,' Trevison cut in. 'I'm doing the things that have to be done around here. If you don't go for it, best thing you can do then is get off the place, and stay off until I'm through. As for talking behind your back – don't fool yourself. You're not worth that kind of trouble. I've said it all to your face to start with.'

'You didn't say anything about me not having any authority to sell my own beef . . .'

'Only because I didn't know about it. I had no idea you were rustling your own herd!'

Washburn was visibly startled. His face colored and he stared hard at Trevison for a long moment; then his eyes shifted, going off into the night. After a time he said, 'That's the way of it, eh?'

'That's the way it is,' Trevison assured him coolly.

Washburn murmured, 'All right, Trevison,' and started for the main house. Several more of the crew rode in, clattering across the hard pack on their way to the corral. A voice, deep in the gloom behind the bunkhouse called, 'Hey, Dub? You goin' to town tonight?'

A dozen steps away Troy Washburn halted. He wheeled slowly around and, for a fraction of time, Trevison thought the man had gunplay in mind. But he said, almost in a friendly tone, 'You're calling the shots, Trevison, and we'll let it go for now. But don't think I'm going to take this lying down. You're making few friends and plenty of enemies in this country. I'm wondering if you'll be big enough to handle it when the chips go down.'

'Don't worry about me,' Trevison answered softly and turned into his quarters.

After the evening meal was over he called Jay Farr aside. 'Send two men to Greer's ranch in the morning. There's twenty-five steers there that belong to us. We're taking them back.'

Farr nodded. 'Be any trouble doing it?'

'No. Greer's getting his money back. How can I get word to Frank Gringras to pay him?'

'Couple of the boys goin' to town tonight. Could send a note to him.'

Trevison wrote out the information and Farr delivered it to the Canaan-bound riders. Afterwards the two of them sat in front of the bunkhouse talking of Tom Washburn, of ranches, of the job that lay ahead of them. Farr was one of the few men Wayne Trevison found it easy to converse with, and he thoroughly enjoyed the old rider's company.

It was late before he realized it. All the lamps were out. Feeling the need for sleep, and rest, he got up. Farr murmured his good night and went off to the bunkhouse. Trevison moved for his own small quarters, thinking back to Troy Washburn's last words, of their underlying threat. He was sitting on the edge of his cot, drawing at a final cigarette, when he heard the tapping at his window.

He swung his attention to that point immediately. In the pale starlight he saw Roxie's face, an indistinct oval beyond the glass. She beckoned to him. A faint forewarning of trouble running through him, he dropped the cigarette to the floor and ground it out. She rapped lightly again. He got up and quietly left the cabin, circling to where she waited.

She was standing in the shadows when he reached her side, smiling softly. She was wearing some sort of night dress, over which she had drawn a thin robe. Her hair was loosely gathered about her head and tied with a ribbon. In the weak light it looked silver.

'I thought that old man would never go to bed!' she said in a husky whisper. 'I've been standing here for hours, it seems.'

Trevison was gruff, impatient with her. 'What do you want, Roxie?'

'To see you,' she replied frankly. 'I was never so glad to see anybody in my life, as yesterday when you came.'

'Why? You and I were through back in Dodge. Besides, you've got a husband now.'

She made a small sound of distaste. 'He's an animal, not a man.'

'But still your husband,' Trevison said. 'You shouldn't be here now, dressed like that.'

She gave him a wide, tantalizing smile. 'Still bother you, don't I Wayne? Makes you think of Dodge and all the good times we had there.'

He said, 'A thousand years ago.'

'But so easily and quickly regained,' she said, moving in close to him. She laid her arms against his chest and leaned her weight upon his tall shape. 'It could be the same as then, Wayne. Just like before.'

The strong attraction of her was a powerful force hammering at his emotions. But he said, 'A thing like this means only trouble. I've got enough of that.'

'But worth it. You know that, Wayne. I can stand anything from Virgil; his jealousy, his possessiveness, even his beatings . . .'

'Beatings?' Trevison echoed.

She drew away from him. Turning her head and drawing back her hair, she showed him a bluish swelling near the cheek bone. 'That's for knowing you in Dodge.'

Trevison shook his head. That would be Virgil's way, all right. He was the kind. A man, ineffectual with other men, feeling their contempt, would take it out on a woman. They all ran true to form. A rider came into the yard, sitting heavy eyed and slack in the saddle. Trevison waited until he had reached the barn and clumped his way to the bunkhouse.

'It's risky here for you,' he said. 'We're stretching our luck. Somebody is bound to see you.'

'Meet me tomorrow then? I'll wait until

Virgil takes his afternoon nap. I can go for a ride.'

Trevison said firmly, 'No, Roxie.'

She pulled away from him, petulant and disappointed. 'Why? Why not? He'll never know. And I can't stand him any longer, Wayne. You've got to help me . . .'

Again Trevison shook his head. There was too much at stake, to risk trouble of this sort with Virgil Washburn. Under other circumstances he might look at it differently. Roxie was a beautiful woman, soft to touch and hold. But not now, not here while he had so many other problems on his shoulders. And besides, she was married.

She said, 'I'll do anything to make you see it my way. You know that. I'm not weak and I get what I want, one way or another.'

'Meaning what?' Trevison asked, his tone going a little stiff.

'Just this. Unless you meet me tomorrow like I ask, I'll tell Virgil about Miles City. The way he feels about you, I think he'd like very much to know about that, about your being a wanted man. It would solve all his problems.'

In the vast stillness that followed her words, Trevison was a tall, rigid figure. He was suddenly hard against a blank wall, facing a problem that offered no solution. He knew this Roxie, knew she would do as she promised, that she would think nothing of upsetting all his plans to obtain her own objective.

"Well?' she pressed softly.

'All right,' he said in a descending tone. 'Where do I meet you?'

'At the picnic grove below the ranch. Three o'clock?'

'Three o'clock,' he repeated.

She reached up, going to her tip toes and kissed him full on the mouth. A moment later she was gone.

TEN

Trevison had a restless night. He was up early and in the saddle long ahead of the crew, striking northward. He wanted a good look at that section of the ranch, and the point at the water hole where the herd would be assembled.

He lifted out of the shallow valley after a short time coming up onto the long-reaching prairie. Here the grass was not so good and this he gave some thought to. He had hoped the grazing in this area would be in better condition, since the entire herd would soon be moving across it. But it was not, and there was nothing that could be done about it; one thing more he could chalk up to Steeg and the Washburn boys. In their negligent short-sightedness, they had permitted the stock, in small broken herds, to graze anywhere and everywhere their fancy took them.

One thing was heartening. The water stand was better than he had anticipated. It was a good two acres across and, walking the bay horse from one shore to the other, he found the bottom firm, though not boggy as such places generally are. The creek was running full, fed further to the north by some underground spring. There would be no water problem at the start of the trek, at least. That was some consolation.

He drifted out of the swale wherein the pond lay like a broad dark mirror under the sun, and rode to the crest of a small hill a mile east. From that point he could see the rollaway of the flat table land in all directions. He had no way of knowing where Washburn's boundaries lay. He assumed he was still within them, but in this huge, unmarked world there was nothing to show where one man's property ended, and another's began.

Coming off the bay, he dropped to his heels and established his directions on a smooth spread of sand with a greasewood twig. He was facing east. To the north, a good five hundred miles away, lay Dodge City and the railhead to which the herd must be delivered. The best route would be up the near center of Texas, along the Western Trail as some called it. It followed the best course and water was assured since the herds crossed the Brazos, the Red, both forks of the Canadian and the Cimarron River – the latter where it laced the Kansas and Indian Territory border.

In the past, Farr had told him, it was customary to start the drive at the Brazos crossing. Trevison studied the lines he had scratched in the sand. This meant they would start out, striking due east until they hit the Brazos, and then swing north up the Trail. The thought occurred to him that, as such, it was a long route; why not slice diagonally across the prairie and join the Trail where it intersected the Red? Several days might be saved in such a move. Every day less on the road meant better beef at the railhead.

He glanced upward to the sun, estimating the time of day. He still had a few hours before he was to meet Roxie. He rode on, changing his direction to a north-easterly route. That was the way the herd would go if he decided to attempt a more direct trail. He kept his watch on the grass, throwing a glance far ahead in search of a stand of green which would indicate a water hole. It never appeared, although the grass did improve after he had dropped off a shelf of mesa into a wide and sweeping valley.

It would be nearly one hundred miles from water at Washburn's extreme north range to the Red River crossing, he figured. Four or five days march for the herd, at least. And three days were about all you could expect cattle to go without a drink. After a while he swung the bay around, heading back. He had spotted no water stands but he was not ready to give up the idea. He would ask Jay Farr about the chances for water further north. One place, if only a small creek, was all they needed to make the shortcut worthwhile.

He swung wide of the ranch on his return, keeping well to the west of it. He ran into several segments of the herd, all moving northward, pointing to the valley where the pond lay. The cattle, as a whole, did not look too good, he noted. But it was soon after winter and little more could be expected. A few days of good grass and water would help considerably. Also, if they had average grazing conditions on the trail, they would arrive at Dodge City in pretty fair condition. He waved to several riders and passed on.

It was a full three o'clock when he reached the grove. It lay below the ranch a few miles.

He had noticed it casually before, but given it no particular attention. It was a thick, circular stand of spreading cottonwood trees clustered about a small spring. In days gone, Tom Washburn and his family, had built a rustic table and several benches there, and quite often held their Sunday picnics in its shaded depths. Once it had been a friendly place where other ranchers also came, and many a trail-weary rider had stopped there to rest his bones and water his horse.

Trevison never entirely off guard, approached from the far side, walking the bay at slow pace through the dense growth. A blur of white dead ahead brought him up short. He threw a sharp glance to that point and saw it was Roxie. When he came softly from the thickets of willows into the open, she wheeled in alarm to face him.

'You frightened me!' she exclaimed, throwing a hand to her throat. 'Was it necessary to come creeping through the bushes like that – like an Indian?'

'Never know who might be around,' Trevison answered, shrugging.

'No one ever comes here anymore,' she said, watching him tether the bay. She was wearing a full flowing riding skirt with a white shirt waist. A small hat perched jauntily upon her head, like a brightly colored straw crown.

The shirt waist fit snugly, accenting the full swell of her breasts; as Trevison sat down beside her on one of the crude benches, she unfastened the top buttons, allowing a greater expanse of white skin to show.

She met Trevison's grave eyes with a faint smile. 'Warm today. If that spring was larger, I'd be swimming right now.'

Trevison allowed his gaze to probe the grove. 'You've been here before?'

'A few times.'

'Family place. Makes a man think of things like that.'

'I was never here with Virgil,' she said, 'if that's what you mean. Having to live with him is enough.'

She laid her hand upon his arm. 'We don't need to make all this small talk, Wayne. Why are we? Old friends like us know each other and talk is such a waste.'

He shook his head. 'This is no good, Roxie. No good for either of us. And dangerous for you.'

'Dangerous?' she scoffed. 'What's Virgil Washburn? A mean, dried-up excuse for a man with a nasty temper.' She paused, shuddered. 'His hands are like snakes. Just as slimy and cold.'

'He's your husband,' Trevison reminded her patiently. 'You picked him. You married

97

him. You didn't have to.'

'No, I didn't have to but I did. All his talk about a big, fine ranch. And money and clothes and trips to the big towns – everything I've always wanted. He made it sound real good.'

'That's not the way it turned out?'

She shook her head. 'No trips to far away places. A ranch he doesn't even own. No money and lots of quarrels. Some men can change quickly, and he is one of those.'

'There's a hitch to most good things,' Trevison said absently. 'You have to take the bad to have the good.'

'But this is all bad, not much good,' she answered, adding, 'but I can take that bad if I can find the good some other place – with you, Wayne.'

She rose swiftly and came around to stand directly in front of him. She put her arms about his neck and drew him in close, burying his face in her bosom. Trevison laid his hands upon the curve of her hips and pushed her gently away. She resisted, holding him tightly.

'Wayne – you don't know, you can't know how I've waited for this.'

Trevison, fighting himself, got to his feet, the movement only bringing her hard against him. He reached for her hands, noting the bruise on her cheek and several more on the snowy white of her shoulders and neck. He said, 'Roxie, you can't do this. . . . I've had nothing to do with another man's wife. I'll not begin now.'

'You will,' she murmured, swaying against him. 'Put your arms around me, Wayne. Hold me – tight.'

He found her hands and broke their tight clasp and tried to step back. She clung to him. And for a moment they stood there, in the shadows of the grove, two figures struggling slightly. It was then Trevison saw the two horses standing a short distance away.

He said, 'Visitors, Roxie,' and pulled forcibly back.

Roxie let her arms fall. There was no fear in her eyes, only a dismay at being thus disturbed. She turned slowly to look.

'My good brother-in-law and his bride-to-be,' she said, her tone tipped with sarcasm. 'Fine time for them to show up!'

Trevison's gaze was upon Halla Greer, reading the shock in her eyes. She pulled her pony about and faced the other way. Troy Washburn rode in closer, a sardonic smile twisting his thin lips.

'Regret the interruption,' he smirked. 'You have a great many talents, Trevison.'

He gave them a down curling smile and

99

swung about to rejoin Halla. They were riding north, toward the ranch, and they continued on.

Trevison watched them leave. Virgil Washburn would have news of this moment before much time elapsed. He said to Roxie, 'Why don't you ride on to town. I'll handle this with Virgil.'

Roxie buttoned her blouse with languid indifference. 'No. Not that way. Let me handle Virgil. I've been through it before.' Then, 'Tomorrow, Wayne?'

Trevison said wearily, 'No, Roxie. Not tomorrow, not again any time. So long as you're married to Virgil.'

She moved toward her horse, swinging her hips. He helped her to the saddle. Settling herself, she smiled down to him. 'Tomorrow – on the other side. Don't forget it, Wayne.'

Standing beside the bench Tom Washburn had built he watched her ride off.

ELEVEN

Two hours later Trevison rode across the hard pack of Triangle W's yard. The crew was still on the range and the only horse in view was Roxie's at the tie rail. Half way to the barn Virgil Washburn's voice, shrill and demanding, ripped through the quiet.

'Trevison! Come over here!'

Trevison half turned in the saddle, giving the man an acknowledging glance, and continued on. He stabled the bay and returned to the yard. For a minute he stood just outside the wide, double doorway, building himself a smoke and thinking about Virgil Washburn. Evidently Roxie had not been as successful as she had anticipated.

He crossed the yard in deliberate steps, presenting himself at the side door of the main house. Before he could knock, Virgil pulled back the door and stepped aside for him to enter. The man was in a high state of agitation, his eyes burning brightly with a wild anger. In one hand he held a pistol, and with this he waved Trevison deeper into the room. Roxie stood in a far corner, her face calm. Trevison closed the door at his heels. In a level voice he said, 'Put that gun away, Virgil.'

Washburn covered him with a murderous glance, his face working with unchecked emotion. 'I will like hell! I'm going . . .'

'Put it away,' Trevison repeated the order. 'You try using it on me and I'll kill you before you can pull the trigger. You know that.'

Washburn gave the weapon a long hopeless look and tossed it onto the table. The defeat of that moment cooling some of the fury that trampled him. A sigh escaped Roxie's throat and a faint, sneering smile came to her lips.

Washburn wheeled away from the table, circling the room, an inner frustration driving him ruthlessly. He was a raging bundle of nerves. He snatched up the short riding crop and stopped in front of Trevison.

'My brother said he saw you with my wife this afternoon!'

Trevison lifted his gaze to Roxie. She nodded, almost imperceptibly. 'He did,' he said.

'What were you doing? What was going on?'

'Your brother told you that, too.'

'He said he saw you standing there – holding her in your arms! He didn't know how long you'd been there . . .'

Trevison, still watching Roxie for his cues, ducked his head. He was trying to say as little as possible, not knowing what Troy had said, nor what explanation Roxie had made of the incident. Virgil Washburn struggled with himself, punishing himself brutally with his own thoughts.

'How long had you been there?'

'Not long,' Trevison murmured.

102

Washburn whirled upon him, his face pushed close. 'My wife said you forced yourself upon her!' The muscles of Virgil's face were writhing in agonised, tight lines.

Trevison saw Roxie's glance slide away, and go searching for something through and beyond the window. Anger stirred within him. He shook it off. It was not worth it. If this was the way she had explained it, then this was the way it would be.

'She said she was there alone, resting. You came along and forced your attentions on her, presuming upon your acquaintance of Dodge City. You deny it?'

Trevison shrugged his wide shoulders. 'You seem to have all the answers.'

Washburn spun away, his face going pale as a jealous fury wracked his body. 'You – you dog!' he screamed. 'Maybe you can come here and take my ranch away from me – but not my wife! Not my wife! You hear that?'

The dam broke suddenly. Washburn lunged across the room and struck out at Trevison with the riding crop.

'You leave her alone! Leave her alone!' he cried, lashing with the whip. 'You stay away from her!'

Trevison stood motionless, taking some of the blows on his shoulders, some on his arms. They hurt but little, and in those moments

103

he was feeling only pity for this man, this small excuse for Tom Washburn. He allowed Virgil's anger to spend itself and then, having enough of it, he seized the riding crop and hurled it across the room. Washburn made a frantic grab for the pistol, lying on the table. Trevison reached it first, and calmly tucked it into the waistband of his trousers. Roxie, silent through it all, watched with indifferent interest.

Trevison turned on his heel for the door. He paused there, throwing a look at the gasping, breathless Virgil leaning weakly against the table.

'Keep your wife inside,' he said. 'Otherwise be with her when she's not.'

He stepped out into the dusk and slanted for his bunk. Remembering Washburn's gun, he flipped back the loading gate and punched out the shells. Afterwards, he dropped the weapon into the dust near the step and moved on.

He washed up with that part of the crew who were in, having some conversation with Farr about the herd. A few places around his shoulders smarted from Washburn's blows with the riding crop. But that bothered him little. It was the necessity that had forced him to stand and take the beating that hurt the most. But even this passed after a time; it

104

was better, he reasoned, that Washburn take his anger out on him than on Roxie.

After the meal was over he called Farr to one side and outlined his thoughts for driving the herd directly to Red River crossing than taking the east route to the Brazos.

Farr puffed at his pipe. 'Well, now, I don't know about that,' he said. 'Pretty risky.'

'Any water that way, to the north?'

Farr said, 'Injun Creek. About fifty miles up.'

'Pretty good stream?'

'Don't know. Never set eyes on it.'

'Tomorrow send a man up there to look it over. Like to know how big the stream is and how much water it's got in it.'

Farr nodded. 'Save a heap of time, goin' that way.'

'Why haven't they used it before?'

'Water for one thing. Sometimes Injun Creek's dry. And raiders. That's the worst thing.'

'Indians or whites?'

'Both, I hear tell. Mostly Injuns.'

Trevison considered this information. After a time he said, 'How long since anybody tried it across there?'

'Five, maybe six years.'

'Tom ever try it?'

Farr shook his head. 'Nope. Always figured it too risky. Things bein' like they was he played it pretty close to the belt. Losin' a herd would have wiped him plumb out, I reckon.'

Trevison said, 'If there's water in that creek, we'll chance it.'

Jay Farr struck a match to his pipe and sucked at the stem. He stared at the flame for a moment, waved it out and flipped it into the yard. 'Don't get me wrong now,' he said slowly, 'but I'm thinkin' that would be a mistake. It's a big chance to take.'

Trevison said, 'With a full crew and all wearing guns, the odds shouldn't be too bad. Main thing is the water. Get a man off for there tomorrow.'

Farr murmured, 'I'll send Jesse Shelton. He's been around long enough to know about what it would take.'

A door at the main house slammed. Virgil Washburn stepped out into the yard, a thin shape in the dim light. Trevison watched him start toward them, pause, bend down and pick up his revolver, lying where Trevison had dropped it. He thrust it into his holster and came on.

He crossed the hard pack, bearing straight for Trevison and Farr. Trevison stiffened, anger stirring through him. The matter of

106

Roxie was concluded so far as he was concerned. He would take no more abuse from Virgil Washburn. Washburn pulled up before them but his attention was on the old puncher.

'You seen anything of Troy?'

Farr shook his head. 'Sure ain't Virg. Been out on the range all day. Why? Something wrong?'

Washburn said, 'I don't know. Looks like most of his clothes are gone. You sure he didn't say anything to you or anybody else around here?'

'Like I told you, I been gone all day,' Farr replied.

'Then, get on your horse and ride in to town and find him,' Washburn said in a clipped tone. 'I want to see him.'

Trevison pushed a step closer to Washburn. 'You want him, you go after him yourself. This man's been working all day, same as the rest of the crew around here.'

Washburn swung his burning gaze on Trevison, hate and fury working his jaws. Words formed on his lips. But he could voice no sound. A moment later he spun about and stalked back to the main house.

TWELVE

Alone in his small quarters Trevison thought of Virgil Washburn's words. Troy was gone. Maybe that was good, possibly it was bad. Around Triangle W he was of no value. Trevison would have viewed any offers of help from him with considerable caution, believing there could be only some hidden reason back of it. But why had he gone, if indeed, he had?

Was he pulling out – giving up, feeling there no longer was anything at Triangle W for him since Trevison had taken over? Was it because his feather bed had turned stone hard and the days of easy come money were over? Or was he drawing off, like some wounded animal to lick his wounds and plan his revenge? In Wayne Trevison's direct and logical mind there had to be a good and valid reason.

He fell asleep thinking of this and he came awake, moments later it seemed, to a furious hammering on his door. He sat bolt upright, reaching automatically for the holstered gun hanging at the bedside. It was a habit he likely would never break.

108

'Trevison!' It was Jay Farr's voice. 'They's trouble!'

Trevison hit the floor and wrenched the door open. The old puncher stood before him, his face gaunt and strained.

'Rustlers! They hit the small herd the boys were bringin' in from the breaks.'

Trevison was pulling on his clothing. 'How many head gone?'

'Don't know. Can't tell yet. They shot Jules up a bit.'

'Bad?'

'Bullet in the shoulder, another in the leg. They're bringin' him in now.'

Trevison came through the doorway at a run, buckling on his gun belt. The bunkhouse lamp was on, light from its windows laying yellow squares in the yard. Four men waited near the corral with saddled horses. Trevison joined them and they whirled away, heading due west.

Farr led the way. It was the stock they had been popping out of the brush, he told Trevison, yelling his words. Jules Bryant and two other punchers were doing the job. They had finally got them out around dark, and driven them a few miles to the north, there bedding them down. Jules had sent one of the riders in for a sack of lunch to tide them over until daylight. The rustlers had struck then.

Trevison cursed under his breath. He leaned lower in the saddle. The horse lengthened his stride and the others, drumming along behind, were pressed to keep up. There was little time to lose. The night was a dark one and the raiders could easily make away with the stolen stock in quick order.

They reached the night camp, a small spot of fire in the long reaching blackness. A man rode out to challenge them, rifle ready across his saddle. Farr yelled, 'It's us, Carl,' and the cowboy trotted in close.

'You see Jules?' he asked.

Farr said, 'No. Reckon we must have missed them on the way. Any more trouble?'

'No. They haven't come back, anyway.'

They rode to the fire. Trevison turned to the rider. 'You alone here?'

The puncher shook his head. 'Jay sent a couple of the boys out to help. They're up with the herd.'

'How was Jules makin' it?' Farr asked then.

'Not good,' Carl replied. 'He was bleeding right smart. We stopped it best we could.'

Trevison was staring off into the darkness. 'Where were you when the rustlers hit?'

'About a mile south.'

Trevison was thinking of Troy Washburn, of his disappearnce from the ranch and the

110

things he had speculated upon. 'You any idea who it was?'

'Nope. I was up at the lead point. Old mossyhorn up there kept trying to stir up the rest, and get them to running. Was having myself a chore trying to settle them down when I heard the shooting. I started back, but the herd was up and milling around so I had a hard time getting through. I finally did and found Jules sitting there in his saddle, all humped over.'

'You didn't see which way the rustlers took off?'

Carl shook his head. 'No, they was gone when I got there. And Jules was in such bad shape I didn't spend any time looking for them.'

Trevison swept the men who had come with him in a single glance. 'Two of you stay here with Carl and the herd. Rest of you come with Jay and me.'

'We'll fan out and do a bit of looking,' he yelled when they were underway. 'I know it's dark and we can't do much about tracks. But walk your horse and listen. Maybe we can pick up the sounds of the cattle moving.'

They separated, branching out like fingers of a hand, and began a search of sorts across the prairie. A long two hours later they had found nothing. Trevison passed the word along and they returned to camp.

'Give it up until daylight,' he said.

One of the riders had dragged in a clump of greasewood and built up the fire. Coffee, made in a lard bucket, boiled over the flames. While it was well watered for the sake of quantity, it was good. For two hours more they hunched about the fire, smoking and taking turns sipping from the bucket.

When the first light began to break Trevison was in the saddle. Farr and the two other riders with him. The rest he left with instructions to push the cattle northward where they could join with the main body of stock. He headed straight for the broken, brushy country that lay to the south and west. He had not covered it before, but he had heard the others speak of it, and realised it would offer quick and adequate cover for the rustlers.

They rode in a wide flung line, traveling slowly. Each man had his eyes on the ground now, searching for telltale tracks. It was difficult. So much stock had passed across the range in recent days that a myriad of prints lay everywhere on the open ground. And where the grass grew thick, there were none at all.

They got their break just before daylight. Trevison saw Farr, riding some distance to his right, haul up and leave the saddle. He watched as the old rider spent a few moments on his hands and knees exploring the ground, then stand up and wave. Trevison relayed the signal and loped his horse to where Farr waited.

'Looks like here's what we been lookin' for,' he said as Trevison pulled up. 'Been a little jag of beef go through here, headin' back into the breaks.'

'That's it,' Trevison said. He touched his horse with spurs and started along the clearly defined trail. They were on the lip of a small canyon in which buckbrier and greasewood and other brush grew in thick, tangled profusion. Trevison pushed along hard. Farr close behind. The other riders had caught up as he could hear them starting the rough descent.

The bottom of the draw was sandy. The tracks were clear and sharp. He paused there, throwing his glance ahead, hoping he might spot motion or some indication of the missing steers' whereabouts. But there was nothing.

He moved on, knowing the cattle could be ten yards – or a mile ahead, it was that difficult to tell. Once he checked the gun at his hip, reassuring himself that the clutching brambles had not dragged it from its scabbard. A good pair of leather chaps

113

would be a welcome bit of clothing here in this world of sharp thorns and tough brush.

It seemed to Wayne Trevison, riding grimly along in the early light, there was little time for anything. In the past, he was never permitted to stay long in any one place because of the imminence of capture; now, it was necessary he move as fast as possible to fulfill his obligation to Tom Washburn – and then move on. And Halla Greer. He wished he might have the chance to explain his position to her, to make her understand his problem. But no such opportunity had been afforded him and likely never would. Time, since that day in Miles City, had become an all important and critical factor in his life.

It seemed to Trevison the brush was getting more dense, more intertwined, more difficult to break through. His horse fought every step, tossing his head nervously; plunging and shying as the briers dug at his hide, and limbs snapped back and lashed him. It came to Trevison that the rustlers were undoubtedly having the same delaying trouble, for the steers would be just as reluctant to travel with any degree of haste. Small draws were gashing the low hills on either side. Trevison began to search them with his eyes. But the tracks of the moving cattle were still plain in the sand before him. They continued, bearing straight ahead.

They broke out into an open place where the ground was fairly smooth. A sharp, upthrusting of rock lifted some ten feet above the surrounding area, and Trevison called a halt. He climbed to the tip of the uprising, and found that from such a vantage point he had a commanding view of the country. From there he spotted the missing cattle.

They were in a dead-end draw, a quarter mile or so to his right. Not more than a dozen head, half of which were lying down, their legs doubled under them in cow fashion. This could mean only one thing; they had been there in their natural corral for some time.

Trevison shouted the information to Farr and the other two riders, and they moved out, following his directions to the arroyo. Trevison kept his eyes roving the land ahead searching for horses and men. He saw nothing, although he remained there on his perch until Farr and the men had hazed the steers out and brought them back up the trail of the main canyon.

Farr paused as the cattle lumbered unwillingly by. 'Any signs of the rustlers themselves?'

Trevison said, 'No,' and climbed down

to his horse. Something was not right. It clawed at his mind, leaving him disturbed and unsettled. Why should the rustlers deliberately drive the stolen stock into a dead end and abandon them? To come back later? That was not reasonable. They had a good enough start to preclude being overtaken and caught. And they would have realized they were leaving a plain trail that could easily be followed to the hidden stock.

He mulled it over the entire distance of the canyon. When they had climbed the steep slope and were once again on the range proper, he said to Farr, 'Jay, none of this makes sense. I've got a hunch we've been played for suckers.'

Farr drew in close. 'How you figure that? We got back the steers.'

'Sure. That's just what they wanted us to do. They had it figured that way. While we were following out an easy trail through the brush, they were driving a bigger herd they cut out last night – in another direction. Probably taking the same route we brought the main herd over so no tracks would show. That jag there in the breaks was just a decoy.'

Farr stroked his mustache. Then, 'Danged if it don't look like you're right! Sure makes sense anyway. They didn't have to stash them critters there in that box.'

Trevison shook his head. 'What we've done is give them another half day's start on us. Half a night and half a day. They're a whole day head, somewhere.'

'Could be anywhere by now,' Farr said morosely. 'Lot of good hidin' country further south.'

Trevison nodded. 'If they've reached there, we can about figure them gone. A few places I think I'll look first though, before we give them up. See you later.'

THIRTEEN

He rode straight to the ranch. The horse was beat, dead tired from the hard trip through the brush-locked canyon, and capable of little more work that day. Also, Trevison wanted to talk with Jules Bryant. He released the bay and roped out a likely looking buckskin from the corral. It took a few minutes to swap gear during which the cook came out and asked: 'You want dinner?' Trevison nodded, remembering there had been no breakfast, other than weak coffee. When it was finished he stopped by the bunkhouse where Jules Bryant lay. The doctor had come and gone,

117

leaving the puncher bandaged and resting easier. He grinned as Trevison entered.

'Dang country's gettin' tough again! You catch up with them rustlers?'

Trevison shook his head. 'Located about a dozen steers hid in the breaks. My hunch is that we were supposed to find them while they drove a big bunch away.'

Bryant stirred, his brows pulling into a frown. 'I been hopin' you'd come by. I think I know who was in that bunch.'

'You get a look at the rustlers?'

'Mighty quick one,' Bryant said. 'There were six or seven of them. Maybe more. They all come yellin' and shootin' at me. But I saw the jasper that plugged me – Jeff Steeg sure as I'm layin' here now! I didn't make no mistake about that big hoss, even in the dark. And maybe one of the others was Troy, but I ain't so sure.'

Trevison got slowly to his feet. He was thinking, where you find Steeg you find Troy. 'You're sure about Jeff?'

'Dead sure.'

The pattern was becoming increasingly clear. Troy and Steeg would not have driven a dozen head of stock into the box canyon and left them there. It was a part of a plan. While a couple of men drove the few deep into the rough country, Troy and Steeg and others

118

struck off in another direction, with a much larger bunch. But where had he taken them? The Hellands, the McMahons, the Greers and Pewter Quinn had received their warnings; yet it did not necessarily follow that they would heed them. And Troy was not an engaging talker.

He nodded to Bryant. 'You take it easy there for a few days. Anybody asks for me, I'll be back when they see me.'

He wheeled out of the bunkhouse and stepped to the saddle. Cutting the buckskin out of the yard, he started at a long lope toward the Helland place. He doubted he would find anything there, but every possibility had to be checked.

It was straight up noon when he reached that ranch. He did not go in close, having little time to spare on words. He circled the structures seeing no stock at all, also finding no sign of any having passed that way. To be doubly sure he rode a few miles further south, to a low-running hogback, from which he could send his search for a much greater distance. But the prairies were empty.

He doubled back for the Greers, intending to do no more than give it a quick inspection, as he had done the Helland spread. But topping the low rise that lay behind the place, he came suddenly head-on into Halla drifting

119

a few steers to the water hole where the main part of the herd grazed. The unexpectedness of his appearance spooked the animals, and they immediately split and began to run.

Trevison grinned at the vexation spreading over the girl's face. He kicked the buckskin into quick action, and pulling free his rope swung, to head off the lead steers. In a few minutes he had them back in line, following out the path that led to the water hole. He coiled his rope and rode to meet her.

Removing his hat, he said, 'Sorry. Didn't mean to break up your drive.'

She nodded coolly. 'Did you check them for brands?'

He said soberly, 'No, ma'am. Should I?'

'I supposed you were still hunting rustlers.'

'Matter of fact, I am.'

'You'll not find them here!'

Trevison said, 'I doubted it myself but a man has to check everywhere. And they might have passed this way.'

Halla thought that over for a moment. Then, 'Who would have been with them? Troy?'

Trevison shook his head. 'Hard to say. Did you see or maybe hear a herd passing?'

'No,' she answered at once. 'But they could have been in the canyon north of us. We wouldn't have seen them or heard them either

HENNEPIN CO.
RIDGEDALE
LIBRARY

06/13/01   1:27PM
000A#4534

BOOK SALES
                  $4.25

ITEMS   10
***TOTAL $4.25
CASH $5.00
CHANGE $0.75

if they went that way.'

She was watching him closely, interest breaking in her eyes. She said, 'I can't understand you, Mr Trevison. One minute I think I like you, the next minute I'm sure I don't. One thing I am positive of is that I believe you are a very great threat to this country.'

'Threat?' he echoed. 'In what way? I'm here just to do a job.'

'But a job that is setting neighbor against neighbor, friends against friends. Maybe even brother against brother.'

Trevison's voice was stiff. 'If that's the result, I'm sorry. What I am doing is a thing that should have been done a long time ago. I have no intentions of stirring up trouble.'

'Does meeting one of the owners' wife come under that heading, too?'

There was a sharpness to her tone Trevison did not miss. He waited a moment then said, 'About yesterday . . .'

She interrupted: 'Yesterday was your business. It is nothing to me.'

Trevison had a brief wish that it was, that she cared about him being with Roxie, and was looking to him for an explanation. A moment later he put aside the hope but he felt inclined to say, 'I knew her back in Dodge City.'

Halla moved her shoulders, a small motion meaning much, meaning little. 'She apparently believes in renewing such old friendships. In a grand way.'

'Not necessarily my wish,' Trevison said.

'That was apparent,' she murmured. Some of the cool briskness had left her and she was now friendlier. 'Troy read one thing in the scene, I read another. All a matter of viewpoint, I guess.'

'Thanks. Now, I'll be moving on.'

She stopped him. 'It's noon. You might just as well drop by the house and eat with us.'

It was common courtesy of the range country. He said, 'Thanks, but another time. There's a few calls I will make before sundown. I hope the invitation will stand.'

'Any time you are passing,' Halla said smilingly.

Trevison swung away, and headed for the McMahon place. There were no steers there. He drifted for a good hour searching for the herd. He found it, and all bore McMahon's Double M brand.

Pewter Quinn was standing and waiting for him on his porch when he rode into the man's yard.

'Step down,' the rancher greeted him.

Trevison shook his head. 'Obliged but I'm

122

looking for some cattle. Thought they might have come by here.'

Quinn said, 'They did – or at least some did. About four o'clock this mornin'. Why?'

Trevison started to say, 'Rustled' but changed his mind. Keeping the lifting temper from his tone, he said, 'Any thoughts as to where they were headed?'

Pewter Quinn rubbed the back of his neck. 'There was a big trail herd movin' north. From Matamoros, somebody said. Likely they threw in with them.'

'Didn't see who was driving the herd?'

'No,' Quinn said. 'Too dark. Anyway, no business of mine. They your steers?'

'Looks that way. How far ahead you think that trail herd is?'

'Not far. Ten, twelve miles maybe.'

Trevison nodded his thanks and swung the buckskin east. He was debating with himself the value of running down the Matamoros herd and checking it for Triangle W beef. Very likely Quinn was right; that's where the stock would be, but by this time it would be so thoroughly integrated with the main herd, that a day would be required to cut them out. And that was something the trail driver would not be in favor of.

He rode slowly on, pondering the problem. If he was figuring right, Troy and Steeg met the big herd, sold them the beef they had driven off the range, collected the money and were now in town enjoying themselves. They would think the steers they had driven into the breaks would cover their trails sufficiently, to throw off all pursuit. Rolling this over in his mind, Trevison came to a conclusion. He cut the buckskin about and drove hard for the road, anger pushing hotly through him. The stock might be gone – but Troy would not enjoy the money for long!

He entered Canaan at a fast trot and bore straight for the Longhorn Saloon. Three horses stood at the rail, none of them familiar. He tied the buckskin alongside them.

Touching the butt of his gun with his finger tips, he pushed through the swinging doors of the saloon into the shadowy interior and halted, allowing his eyes to adjust themselves. Except for three riders sitting at a back table playing a desultory game of cards, and the bartender, the place was empty.

He walked to the bar, watching the alarm rise in the man's round eyes. He said, 'You remember me, friend. I'm the man you steered into Jeff Steeg's arms the other night.'

Trevison's tone laid its chill upon the man. He looked down, nervously wiping at the shelf behind the bar. 'I don't reckon I . . .'

'I was going to drop back and take you

apart then. But I figured it wasn't worth the effort – until now . . .'

The card game stalled. The three cowboys were watching Trevison. He swung his gaze to them, hard and arrogant. One by one they looked away. The bartender said in a breathless way, 'What do you mean by that?'

'Where's Troy Washburn? Where's Jeff Steeg?'

The barkeeper shook his head. 'Ain't here.'

'I can see that,' Trevison gritted. 'Where can I find them?'

'I don't know . . .' the man whined.

Trevison reached over the bar and grabbed the man by the front of his shirt and jerked him forward. His eyes popped wide with fear and his mouth fell open.

'Where are they? You've got five seconds before I crease your skull with my gun barrel!'

'Abilene,' the man gasped. 'They said Abilene – they was goin' there.'

Trevison pulled harder, dragging the bartender higher up onto the bar. 'Where in Abilene?'

'I don't know, mister! Honest I don't! Maybe the Silver Dollar. I've heard Jeff talk about that place.'

Trevison pushed the man away. He slammed hard against the back bar. Bottles clattered and some fell.

Trevison said coldly, 'Now, we're even for the other night. Next time you head a man into trouble think about it first. It could get you killed later.'

He pivoted on his heel, covering the card players with a sliding glance, and walked to the doorway. Abilene. That was the answer and it figured right. Troy and Steeg with money to throw around, would be in one of two places; either the Longhorn or in Abilene. And they were not at the former.

He mounted the buckskin and rode him to the livery stable. The horse was tough but he would not be able to stand up under a fast run to Abilene and back. Leaving him there, he rented a stalwart gray and within a half hour, was heading south. The afternoon was fading, but not Wayne Trevison's anger. Indeed, when he rode into Abilene, his temper had built itself into a hard, reasonless fury against Troy Washburn.

FOURTEEN

He made his way along the street, squirming with the night's traffic until he located the Silver Dollar Saloon. It was a two-storied, sprawling affair. He circled it to its side door. Dismounting there, he tied the gray to a cottonwood growing in the yard. Pausing for a minute to be certain he had not been followed, he climbed the short landing and let himself inside.

He halted again, letting the shadows drain from his eyes and accept this new and sudden change. He was in a short hallway that came off the end of the bar, and after a moment, he followed it out.

The place was packed and no one saw him arrive. The line at the long, mahogany bar was shoulder to shoulder and three bartenders worked pouring drinks and keeping the counter clean. The barkeeper paused in front of Trevison. 'Yours, friend?'

'Beer,' Trevison said and watched the man glide smoothly away. The beer came sliding back to him and he laid his coin on the counter.

Over the rim of his glass he studied the crowd, ticking it off as best he could. But it was a shifting, buoyant mass and he had difficulty. He found Jeff Steeg first. The big puncher was at the far end of the bar; his back half turned, one elbow hooked on the counter, talking with a woman.

Trevison swung his attention then to the tables, to the card games in progress. There he would most likely find Troy Washburn. One by one he checked them and when he was done, he had not located the man. The bartender came up again.

Trevison laid his hand across his glass. 'Where's the big game tonight?'

The barkeeper ducked his head to the left, to the doors past the end of the bar, behind Steeg. 'Back rooms.' He cast a doubtful look at Trevison. 'High stakes for a puncher. You figure to set in?'

Trevison shook his head. 'Might,' he murmured and pushed out into the milling crowd.

He circled wide around Jeff Steeg, wanting no trouble from that point at this particular moment. There were two doors behind the bar. He opened the first quietly and saw three men at a round table, their guns lying in sight as they played silently. A fourth man sitting astride a chair and leaning on its back, watching with close interest. He did not look up as Trevison made his examination. Troy was not in there.

He moved to the next door and pushed it open. Smoke hung about an overhead lamp, and the sharp click of chips was the lone sound that greeted him. Five men were at the table and one of those was Troy. He sat with his back to the door. Trevison slid softly into the room and one of the players, a man with thin, sallow features and smoking a black cheroot, flicked him with only casual interest, then went back to his game.

Trevison drifted quietly up to a point just behind Washburn. He was carefully probing the faces of the others in the small box-like room, assessing their possible reaction to the move he would soon make. He noted then there was no other door besides the one he had come through and the single window was high and small, of no use as an exit.

Trevison's gaze came back to the game. The pot was a heavy one, coins and currency piled high in the center of the table. It was the final round of cards. The man with the cheroot drew one. Next man dropped out, Washburn called for two. The fourth player drew a single and the last stood pat. Washburn checked the bet and the player who had stood pat tossed a gold eagle into the wager. All players called, and on the laydown, Washburn was high man.

Trevison watched him drag the bills and coins in. When he reached into his shirt pocket for his roll and had folded the addition to it, Trevison leaned over his shoulder and plucked it from his fingers. Washburn yelled his surprise. One of the players exclaimed, 'What the hell!'

Trevison, hand resting suggestively on the butt of his gun, back stepped to the door. Placing his shoulder against it, he thrust the money into his pocket. Washburn had scrambled to his feet, eyes wild, mouth working convulsively.

'Just all of you stay seated and nobody will get hurt,' Trevison said coolly. 'Make no sudden moves. This is no holdup, otherwise I'd be taking all of your cash. I just came after the money this man forgot to turn in after he sold some cattle of mine.'

'Why, you . . .' Washburn began hotly.

'Go ahead,' Trevison invited coldly. 'Let's hear it.'

But Washburn had no more to say. He watched Trevison with a hard and narrow gaze, white with anger.

Trevison said, 'I want no trouble from any of you. But follow me through this door and you've got it.'

He reached for the knob, pressing into his hip, and turned it. He pulled back the door, eyes drilling into Washburn. 'Don't come after me, Troy,' he warned softly and stepped into the main part of the saloon.

There were the immediate sounds of hurried confusion beyond the door, but it did not open. His threat was holding good – at least for a time. He ducked away into the

130

jamming crowd endeavoring to move fast but unobtrusively for the batwings, clear across the room. He was half way there when Troy Washburn's voice yelled: 'Jeff! Trevison's out there somewhere! Hey, Steeg!'

Trevison worked his way through the closely packed shapes. He kept his head down, moving steadily. He would like to stop and locate Steeg and Washburn, and thus get a better idea of his chances. But common sense told him it was wiser to keep his face hidden and press on.

Grim humor was moving through him as he recalled the shocked amazement in Troy Washburn's eyes when he had taken the money from his fingers.

'Steeg!' Washburn's voice again lifted above the din. 'You see him yet? Jeff! Where are you?'

The big puncher made no audible answer and this disturbed Trevison. If the man had replied, he might have been able to pinpoint his position in the crowd.

'Over there! Over there by the doorway!' Washburn sang out suddenly.

A man next to Trevison wheeled and stared. He said, 'This one?' and grabbed Trevison's arm. Trevison, seeing the swinging doors only half a dozen steps away, struck out viciously, driving a solid fist into the man's belly. The

131

grip on his arm relaxed at once. He pushed for the doorway, hearing Troy's insistent yells grow behind him, and the clamor of the crowd lift with them. Another man loomed dead ahead and then faded quickly aside as Trevison drew his gun and bore straight on. The doors, at last, were close. Another yard and he shouldered through them and cut sharply right – coming hard into Jeff Steeg.

Trevison had the advantage of the moment. Surprise was with him. He had a fragment of time in which to set himself and swing. The blow caught Steeg on the side of the head, too high to be decisive. But its tremendous force rocked the big man to his heels and off balance and sent him staggering away and off the porch.

The crowd was boiling through the doorway and out into the street. Shouts, laughter, the shrill cry of a woman as unwelcome hands took advantage of the situation. Trevison crowded Steeg, driving him back before he could get squared away. There was no time to fight now.

Grim and silent, he drove his fist into Steeg. The man's grunts plain in his ears. A gun crashed through the night, coming from somewhere in the jostling crowd. Trevison thought, *here comes the law now*, and lashed out savagely. He had to break clear of Steeg and get away, at any cost. But Steeg was fighting back. Trevison rushed the puncher, striking with all he had. Time had again run out. He had to get away; he could not afford to let any law officer arrest him, regardless of the charge. Steeg's face was suddenly close before him, his eyes alight with hatred and fury. Blood smeared his features, trickling from his flattened nose and crushed lips.

'Got you, Trevison!'

'Not yet, Jeff,' Trevison murmured. He drove his left wrist deep into the man's midsection. Breath exploded from Steeg's mouth in a whistling gasp. He buckled forward. Trevison, timing it perfectly, caught him with an upswinging uppercut that connected squarely. Pain shot through Trevison's arm, all the way to his shoulder and he had a moment's fear that he had broken his hand. Steeg reeled away drunkenly into the murky darkness, falling sideways like a hewn tree. Trevison, dragging deep for wind, dodged off to his right, toward the protective blackness of a building standing hard by. The mouth of an adjoining alleyway opened up and, seeing starlight at the far end, he started down it at a hard run. Back of him in the street the shouts increased. A man, nearer than the others called, 'Halt! Lest I shoot!' in a sharp, commanding voice.

The end of the alley was near. Trevison ducked and ran on. The bullet cracked in the narrow canyon between the two buildings; the sound a deafening, shattering wallop in his ears. He reached the end and swung left, going further away from the Silver Dollar, toward the gray horse waiting for him there. Boots were rapping along the hard-packed ground of the alleyway, and drawing closer. An open doorway of the building he had just rounded showed darkly in the pale shine. He swerved toward it, grabbed the knob and jerked hard. The door came shut with a slam. Another two strides and he had reached the far corner of the structure and was around it and heading back for the street.

'In that old store!' a voice yelled behind him. He grinned mirthlessly. They had taken the bait. 'I heard the door slam shut!'

'Get around front, somebody!'

Trevison entered the street, walking swiftly to where several horses waited at a tie rail. Men were pounding up the length of the vacant building. The crowd had mostly trailed through the alleyway, and now were gathering at the opposite end. Standing there with the horses, like a rider who apparently had just arrived, or was leaving, Trevison called to the nearest man, 'What's going on around here?'

'Got a jasper holed up in there,' the man

134

replied breathlessly. He swung his sweaty face toward the back. 'We got him blocked here, Marshal!'

'What'd he do?' Trevison asked, pulling the reins of a little buckskin free.

'Hanged if I know,' the fellow answered. 'Everybody's just tryin' to catch him. Somethin' he did back there in the saloon, I reckon.'

Trevison swung up into the saddle. If his luck would only hold for another few seconds, just until he could reach the darkness beyond the street, he would have done it.

'Come out of there!' A man was yelling into the empty building as he crossed the street. 'We got you covered!'

Trevison reached the opposite side and rode into the deep shadows of another alleyway. Following this path eventually brought him to a point opposite the Silver Dollar. For a long minute he watched that structure, seeing the gray waiting patiently for him at the side tie rail. There were few people in the saloon, none on the porch or in the yard. The majority of Abilene was down the street where the demands for him to leave the empty storehouse were growing more insistent.

'Smoke him out!' a voice yelled. 'Throw a little fire in there, Marshal. That'll bring him out!'

Trevison grinned in the darkness. He cut the buckskin back and traveled another hundred yards north along the street. There, well beyond the flare of light, he crossed over, doubled back and came into the yard beyond the saloon. He exchanged the buckskin for the gray and swung quietly out of the town for Canaan.

A mile away he paused to study the lurid glow hanging over Abilene. Apparently they had gone ahead with the idea of smoking him out, but somehow the fire must have gotten out of hand.

Around eleven o'clock that next morning Trevison rode into Canaan. He was weary and hungry. He pulled up at the stable, dismounted and walked the tired gray inside. The hostler came from the rear to meet him, took the gray and moved to exchange the gear to the buckskin, now rested after a night's sojourn in the barn. When he was back, Trevison paid the toll and returned to the street. He headed first for the bank.

Frank Gringras came to the door to meet him, watching him silently as he looped the leathers over the bar. When Trevison wheeled toward him he said, 'Man, you look beat. Anything wrong?'

Trevison dug into his pocket. 'No, just

collecting for some cattle.' He handed the roll of bills to the banker. 'Add this to the Washburn account. Troy sold some steers.'

Gringras looked closely at him but Trevison's face was closed, showing nothing. Gringras shrugged and turned about. 'Wait until I make a receipt.'

Trevison leaned against the door frame, letting his glance travel the town. Halla Greer came into view, straight and tall on her little pinto horse, and pulled up at the general store. Trevison watched her with interest.

'Better get yourself some sleep,' Gringras advised, thrusting the slip of paper into his hand. 'Things all right at Washburn's? You going to start the drive soon?'

'Soon,' Trevison murmured and walked away.

He slanted across the street to a small shop where the barber plied his trade. Trevison sank into the hard, straight-backed chair and as the man drew a checked apron tight around his neck, said, 'Haircut. Shave. And don't wake me up if I fall asleep.'

Only moments later, it seemed, the barber was gently shaking his shoulder. 'Finished. I let you alone for an hour, long as I could. Now I got another customer.'

Trevison felt much better. The few minutes sleep had taken the edge off his weariness.

He paid his bill and went back into the street. Halla Greer's pony was now in front of the bank and as his glance came to a rest upon it, the girl came from the building and mounted up. She swung back up the street and Trevison sauntered out to meet her.

She pulled up before him, watching him with her serious, half-smiling eyes. 'Find your rustlers, Mr Trevison?'

He said, 'I did.'

'Just now get back?'

He nodded. 'Rode in an hour ago.'

'Must have been a long ride,' she observed thoughtfully.

'It was that,' he agreed, 'and a hungry one. Would you allow me to turn your invitation around and ask you to have dinner with me? Here at the café.'

She smiled quickly. 'Of course. I had planned to eat in town today.'

She dismounted and he led the pinto back to where the buckskin waited. Trevison's towering shape made the girl's slight figure seem small, almost childlike against it.

They reached the restaurant and Trevison held back the door for her to enter, following himself. Inside he pulled up short, the sparse form of Sheriff George Bradford blocking his way.

Bradford was an old man, of Tom

Washburn's generation. He had a seamed, deeply-grooved face only partially hidden by a goatee-style beard and full flowing mustache. His hair was almost snow white and it hung long, shoulder length beneath a black, flat crowned hat.

He said unsmilingly, 'Been expecting you, Crewes.'

Trevison settled himself gently, all the old mistrust of men wearing stars coming to the fore. He was worried about this totally unexpected encounter with the law. It disturbed him, thinking of what Halla Greer might hear and see. And the possibility of her getting hurt. He threw a quick, sideways glance at her, seeing the frown at the name, Crewes, which Bradford had used, brought to her eyes.

He said coolly, 'Little pressed for time, Sheriff. Anyway, why should I drop by to see you?'

'Rule of mine,' Bradford rumbled. 'Always like to know who's in my town. Understand that's your name – Crewes. Jim Crewes.'

In the hush of the room, tight with tension, Trevison said, 'They call me that.'

'Your real name?'

Trevison waited out a full minute, calculating the pressures. Under the direct, probing gaze of the sheriff he said, 'There anything wrong with it?'

Bradford eyed him in a dissatisfied way. 'You look a little familiar. We ever met before?'

Trevison shook his head. 'Don't think so.'

He brushed by the man then, cutting him out. Taking Halla by the arm he guided her to a back table and seated her. Pulling out a chair for himself he settled down, tension drawing his nerves taut. He lifted his glance to Bradford, who stood there watching him with crimped eyes, while he sought to justify the suspicion that flowed through him. A minute later he shrugged, drew back the door and walked into the street.

Trevison, only then, turned his attention to Halla. Her face was a study and he knew she was having her deep wonderment about him, about the name Bradford had used. He said, 'I'm sorry about it. About the sheriff.'

The waitress came up and they ordered, Trevison asking for coffee to be served at once. When they each had their cups Halla said, 'Which is your name – Crewes or Trevison?'

He said, 'Trevison.'

'Are you wanted by the law?'

He said, 'Yes,' and watched something move into her gray eyes, a dullness that told of her dismay.

140

The waitress returned with their plates and no more was said of it. For a few minutes they ate in silence, and when they were ready for pie and a final cup of coffee, she lifted her gaze to him.

'You said you found the rustlers. Does that mean Troy?'

Trevison smiled. 'Not hardly right to call a man who takes some of his own cattle a rustler, I reckon.'

'But he had taken some and sold them, and was going to keep the money. Like those he sold my father.'

'Yes,' Trevison said. He dug the makings out of his pocket and rolled a smoke.

She watched him light it. Then, 'That's where you've been, getting the money from Troy?'

Trevison slanted a sharp glance at her. He said, 'Gringras talks too much.'

She laughed lightly. 'Don't blame him too much. I wormed it out of him.'

She was silent after that and he knew she was wondering about him. There were things she knew, others she assumed; now she was having a hard time putting them together and making them jibe in the nice, perfect way women like to have such things fit. She had talked with Gringras, therefore she knew he had followed Troy and collected money from him. And then he turned it in to the banker. Yet, he was a man under an assumed name; a man wanted by the law for some crime or another. It simply was not compatible. A criminal riding all night to turn back money he could have easily gone on with.

'Don't let any of this disturb you,' he said with a grin. 'There's an answer to it all.'

She started at the sound of his voice. She said, 'I'm sure of that.' A moment later she added, 'You should smile like that more often. You always look so grim! Smiling does something for you – breaks those bitter lines around your mouth.'

Trevison shrugged. 'Man needs something to smile about, or for, these days. Maybe you're that something.'

She viewed him archly, words forming upon her lips. But she passed them by, giving him instead her serious smile. She rose, and he got quickly to his feet.

'Time I was leaving. Are you riding back to Triangle W now?'

'With you, I hope,' he said.

He dropped three silver dollars onto the table and they walked out into the strong, warm sunlight. They turned toward their horses and Trevison saw, in that instant, the shape of Bradford come from his office and slant toward them. At once anger stirred through him, building its strong, pushing impatience. He halted, saying softly, 'Go ahead, Halla. This may be trouble.' But she refused. She stopped, as did he. Bradford strolled up, and came to a halt in the center of the street, his gaze on Trevison.

'Just thought I'd ask again. You sure we never met before?'

Temper plucking at his self control, Trevison held a tight rein on his words. From the corner of his eye he could see Halla, watching him with anxious interest. He said, 'I still doubt it, Sheriff. Never been in this country.'

'Where you from then if this ain't your country?'

Trevison waited out a long moment, letting the man know he did not appreciate the question which, by all rights, he could let pass. He said, 'Lots of places.'

'Any place special?'

Anger snapped in Trevison. He laid a cold glance on Bradford. 'Sheriff,' he said in deliberate calmness, 'you don't know me. You never met me before. You can believe that. Now, let's get something understood. You got some charge you want to trump up against me, bring it out and let's hear it. Otherwise stay away from me!'

Bradford stared at Trevison, his faded old

eyes level and undisturbed. He shook his head. 'Sure son, sure,' he murmured and moved away.

Trevison watched him leave, heat running slowly from him. A warning began to lift; Bradford was suspicious. He knew something, probably that Crewes was not his real name. And maybe, stored back there in his memory, was the recollection of a face on a reward dodger. Likely that was what he had been doing after he left the restaurant, checking through his stack of posters at his office. Apparently he had not found it, or he would not still be uncertain of his ground.

He was aware then of Halla, waiting there beside him. She said, 'We'd better start . . .'

He nodded, 'Of course. I'll say again I'm sorry. The sheriff seems to have something on his mind.'

She turned to him, her face still. 'Are you worried about it?'

'I never worry,' he smiled, 'only try to be careful.'

FIFTEEN

The first miles were quiet ones. Halla was wrapped in her thought and Trevison, not wanting to disturb her, let her have her way. He confined himself to considering Sheriff Bradford and the possible danger that might lie at that point.

They left the loose, powdery dust of the road and struck out across the grass of the prairie. Off to the right, a bright splash of lighter green marked the location of a spring, with its inevitable stand of cottonwood trees. Halla turned to him. 'It's hot. Shall we rest a bit in the shade?'

Trevison nodded his agreement and they swung toward the trees. Reaching there, they stepped down, and he led the horses to water. Halla found a seat on a rotting log and when he came back, she did not face him.

Trevison held his peace. She was, he realized, having her own deep and fierce struggle over him; trying to place him in his proper niche in her mind, and decide her feelings for him. Women were like that; a man was good or he was bad – and there was little compromising middle ground. Thus Trevison kept silent, allowing her to come to her own conclusions.

He could not keep his steady glance from her, and the thought of her passing from his life was an unwelcome one. There was something about this woman that reached out and took firm hold upon his consciousness. He loved her.

He stirred suddenly, catching himself at his own thoughts. The slightest groan escaped his lips. *What a fool I am to think of things like that! Me – a man with no future, no home, no place to go – nothing!*

'You said they wanted you. Is – is it for something bad? Something really serious?' she asked.

He said, 'Murder. I killed a sheriff.'

'Murder?' she echoed faintly. 'Just like that – murder. No reason? No cause?'

He said. 'That's what they called it. It's what the reward dodgers with my picture on them say; "wanted for murder".'

'But was it?'

He shook his head. 'No.'

A small whisper of relief slipped through her lips.

He said, 'I told this story once, back in Montana. Nobody believed it except one man, and he couldn't help.'

'Go on, Wayne. I want to hear it.'

He dropped his glance to his hands, fisted into hard knots across his knees. Slowly he released them, spreading his fingers wide as the tenseness decreased. 'I had a brother, four years younger than myself. My folks were killed by Indians when I was ten years old. A rancher by the name of Goodman took us in and we grew up there. That's where I met Tom Washburn. He was the foreman for the outfit – and the only father I can remember.

'After Tom left Montana we stayed on at Goodmans. But my brother got mixed up with a couple of punchers. There was some trouble. A man was killed in a holdup. My brother came and told me all about it. While he was guilty of being with the two men, he was not there at the time of the killing. I sent him to stay with a friend of ours, until I could get things straightened out with the sheriff.

'I went to see the sheriff, a friend of mine, I thought. I told him the story. He said if I would persuade my brother to give himself up, he would see he got a fair deal. They already had the actual killers. Maybe he would get a short time in jail for being a part of the gang, but not for any murder charge. I talked my brother into it because I was convinced it was the right thing to do. I didn't want him dodging around the rest of his life with – a price tag on his head. He came

147

in with me to the sheriff and turned himself in. Next day he was dead.'

'Dead?' Halla echoed. 'Dead?'

Trevison nodded slowly. 'The sheriff told me he had tried to escape. His deputy backed him up. They were moving him to another jail in the next town. For safe keeping, they said. I got there only a few minutes after it happened. He still had the handcuffs around his wrists. And his feet were roped under his horse. The bullet was in his back.'

There was horror in Halla's voice. 'But if he was handcuffed and tied to his horse, how could he . . .'

Trevison said, 'Same thing I asked the sheriff. He said he guessed I was a little too smart and went for his gun. I shot him before he could draw.'

Halla considered this for a time. Then, 'How did you get away, with the deputy there?'

'He was on my side. I went back to the town with him, thinking he would back up my story of what happened. Instead, he said I had tried to spring my brother free, and in the shooting, the sheriff had killed my brother; and I had then put a bullet into the sheriff. It was a fine, old double cross.'

'You were able to break jail later?'

'This friend of mine, the only one that

believed my story, smuggled me a gun. I managed the rest.'

Halla said nothing for a time, thinking over what he had said. Then, 'Of course it was no more than self-defense. Did you ever think of going back and trying to clear your name? There must be some way it can be done.'

'How? Every lawman between here and Miles City is just looking for the chance to collect rewards like the one on my head. Not to mention the bounty and plain cowboys. I'm worth a thousand dollars, dead or alive, to any of them.'

She shuddered. 'But you can't go on forever like this, looking over your shoulder, wondering if there's somebody on your trail. Like there in town today. I could see the change come over you when Bradford stopped you. You were different, a man I'd never before seen. You made me think of a wolf backed into a corner, ready to fight it out to a finish.'

He grinned. 'That's a good way to put it; a wolf at bay.' The smile faded. 'One they'll never collect bounty on,' he added grimly.

'But you can't . . .' she began, lifting her hands in a palm upwards gesture. 'There must be some way to change it.'

Trevison shook his head. 'I've thought about them all. Even tried for a while to

149

do it but it's my word against the deputy's and they listen to him. Only answer I've ever found is to keep moving. Maybe Mexico one of these days.'

'It wouldn't end there. Somebody would recognize you eventually and bring you out. Maybe dead, across the back of a horse.'

He shrugged. 'Something I would have a little say-so about. Man doesn't follow this trail for as long as I have without learning to look out for himself.'

'But you can't do that forever.'

Trevison said, 'I've managed so far,' and got to his feet. He stood there, tall, wide shouldered in the sunlight, looking off into the far reaches of the prairie. He half turned and found her close beside him, looking up into his face. His arms went around her at once, drawing her into their strong circle, pressing her against him. His mouth found her lips, the solid pressure of it bringing a faint gasp from her.

'We – had better go,' she managed after a moment.

He released her at once, moving away wordlessly. There was no apology in him, no regret and he made no comment. He merely walked to where the horses waited, gathered up the trailing reins, and led them to where she stood. He helped her mount and then swung onto the buckskin.

They had covered a mile when he broke his silence. Drawing in close beside her, he laid a hand upon hers. 'We will forget what happened back there. It's not in the cards much as I would like to think so. I can't drag you into my troubles.'

'Two people often do better solving a problem than one,' she murmured.

He shook his head. 'Not this kind of problem. My mistakes are my own. I'll not have you or anybody else paying for them. Now, we'll talk of other things.'

She started to raise some protest, make some objection to his strong words, but thought better of it. After a time she said, 'How are things at the Washburn place? Will you soon be ready for the drive to Dodge City?'

'Shouldn't be too long,' he replied. It was idle talk, both of them skirting the subject of his past, his future. 'Farr thinks we should be ready in a week or two.'

'What about Troy? I know he has given you a lot of trouble. Will he ever change, you think?'

Trevison said, 'Probably. He's wild and spoiled. Give him a little more time, maybe he will come out of it.'

She looked at him sharply. 'You are saying

151

that for my benefit! I doubt if you believe it. Don't spare him because of me. It has always been a fond dream of my father's that someday Troy and I would marry. But it's no desire of mine and I think now he has changed his mind about it.'

'A thing I'm pleased to hear,' Trevison stated.

Halla said, 'Oh,' in a wondering sort of way. When he said no more she added, 'You don't think much of Virgil either, I guess.'

'He's different. That I will say.'

'And his wife . . .' Halla remarked with a teasing laugh. Immediately she sobered, seeing he did not consider it so lightly.

'I'm sorry for her,' Trevison said. 'What lies ahead for her as his wife can be nothing short of hell and misery.'

They were climbing the last rise, reaching the crest. Triangle W's scatter of buildings lay before them in the afternoon sunlight.

Trevison said, 'We'll stop for a cool drink and then I'll see you home.'

'See me home?' she repeated with a laugh. 'Why, nobody's done that for me since I was a child. But I like it.'

They rode down the gentle slope at a leisurely pace. As they drew closer and things began to grow more distinct and take shape, Trevison saw several of the men in the yard, one of them Jay Farr. They were standing a few yards from the main house, half way to the corral. The cook was on the kitchen step, leaning against the doorframe, his attention, too, focused on the house. As they rode deeper in Trevison heard the shrill voice of Roxie and the stronger demanding tones of Virgil Washburn.

Trevison pulled up, Halla close to his side. Farr came over to meet them, his long face sober. Roxie's scream lifted in volume. And there was the dull thud of a striking object.

'What's going on in there?' Trevison asked.

Farr touched the brim of his hat to Halla and nodded. Then, 'Been that way for more'n a hour. Her yellin' like that and him a cussin' and hittin' her with something. Started in there myself a dozen times, but then allowed as how I got no call to interfere in a family squabble.'

Trevison glanced back to the house. Farr was right, of course, but he did not know how much of Roxie's crying he could stand before he would be compelled to take a hand.

Halla said, 'I think I'd better ride on. Don't bother to come along.'

The sudden flat crash of a gunshot rocked the yard.

Trevison came off his horse in one long leap. He sprinted for the side door. It burst

153

wide and Virgil Washburn, blood streaming down his shirt front, staggered into the open. He fell almost at once, his fingers clutching tightly the riding crop.

A moment later Roxie appeared. Her hair was down about her waist, her upper clothing in shreds. Her face and bare shoulders were covered by livid, red welts. She looked dazedly about the yard and seeing Trevison standing there, gave a little cry. Dropping the gun from her fingers, she ran sobbing to him.

Roxie threw herself into Trevison's arms.

'I didn't want to do it – but I couldn't stand any more of his beatings!'

From his knees alongside Virgil Washburn's body, Farr said, 'He's dead.'

Halla Greer dismounted and moved quickly to where Trevison was holding Roxie loosely against his chest. She laid a hand on the girl's shoulder.

'Why not come home with me, Mrs Washburn?'

Roxie half turned and faced her. She shook Halla's hand away. 'No! No! I'll stay here – with Wayne.'

Farr had swung to one of the men standing nearby. 'Ride into town and get Bradford. Get the coroner, too.' The cowboy wheeled to comply, and Farr motioned to another rider. 'Get a blanket out of the bunkhouse and throw it over him. Don't go meddlin' with nothin' now, specially that whip. That shows it was self-defense.'

Roxie had quieted some. The hysterical crying had diminished and now she stood silent. Halla had not gone yet. Trevison pushed Roxie away gently. She reached into a pocket and produced a wisp of white and dabbed at her swollen eyes.

'Hadn't you better go with Halla?' Trevison suggested. 'I'll have the boys hitch up the buggy. You will be better off with her.'

Roxie stared at the blanket shrouded form on the ground. 'Is he dead?'

'He's dead,' Trevison answered soberly.

The girl shuddered. 'I'll never forget the look on his face when I pulled the trigger. Never – not if I live to be a hundred years old!'

'Don't think about it now,' Trevison said softly. 'Go with Halla.'

Roxie swung then to Halla Greer. She said, 'Why? I'm all right. I don't need her help. Nor anybody else's. I want to stay here where I belong – and with you, Wayne.'

Trevison saw the stillness move into Halla's eyes. Without speaking, she turned and walked away. Trevison started to follow, to go after her. Roxie threw her arms around him, holding him back.

'Wayne! Stay with me – don't leave me now.'

He watched in silence as Halla swung to her saddle. When she rode by, not a half dozen yards distant, she held her gaze straight ahead, and he could see her face was devoid of expression. Trevison felt a heaviness settle within him then, a great hopelessness that knew no depth. He followed the spotted pony as it climbed the far slope, Roxie babbling at his side about the two of them; how they could now be together and own this ranch and times would be for them as they once had been, long ago. But he was only half listening.

Finally he said, 'Hush, Roxie.'

He reached down and picked her up, and carried her into the house. Looking back over his shoulder as he passed through the doorway, he had a last glimpse of Halla just topping the ridge and going out of sight.

Sheriff Bradford arrived accompanied by Dr Skillings who also served as town coroner. As Farr predicted Bradford and the physician declared it to be a matter of self-defense, and Roxie was exonerated of any wilful blame.

Bradford said then, 'You want us to take him in to town?'

Farr spoke up. 'Reckon not, George. We'll bury our own dead. Tom would've wanted him put right along side himself and the

156

missus, there in the family plot back of the ranch. Obliged to you though if you'll pass the word around and tell the preacher to come out.'

'All right,' the sheriff answered. 'What about Troy? He know about this yet?'

Farr shook his head. 'He ain't been around for several days. Thought maybe he was in town and you'd tell him.'

Bradford looked thoughtful. 'I don't think he's in town, Jay. Leastwise, I sure haven't seen him lately.'

Trevison, keeping out of the conversation up to this point said, 'Try Abilene. The Silver Dollar saloon.'

Bradford swung a quick, inquiring glance at Trevison but he made no comment. Farr broke in. 'I'll send a man over there right away. Tell the folks the services'll be about dark. That'll give Troy time enough to get here.'

Bradford nodded and climbed into his buggy. Dr. Skillings came out of the house where he had been attending Roxie.

'Gave her a little something to make her rest. And I put some ointment on those bruises. Virgil must have been out of his mind, doing a thing like that.'

'Never know what's inside a man,' Bradford observed as they walked away.

Troy was not in Abilene. The puncher Jay
Farr had sent for him returned the next day
and said he had tried not only the Silver
Dollar, but every other gambling house in
town as well. And in addition, he and the
marshal had checked at the hotels and livery
barns. One man said Troy had left town after
some sort of ruckus a few nights before. He
did not know where he was headed.

The services were conducted by the
minister just as the sun was dropping over
the rim of the range. There were a few people
from town, and Halla Greer and her father.
None had come for Virgil's sake; he had no
friends. All were there out of respect for Tom
Washburn and his wife. Virgil was buried in
the small, fenced-in plot of ground reserved
for such purposes on a slight knoll behind the
ranch buildings.

Trevison stood near Roxie through it all,
there being no one else for her to lean upon.
Twice he glanced at Halla but she kept her
eyes down; and when it was all over, she
paused to murmur her condolences to Roxie
and then left without looking at him.

After supper that night, which he ate with
Roxie in the dining room of the main house,
she said, 'I'm going away, Wayne. Leaving
for a while. Will you come with me?'

Impatiently, he said, 'Of course not. You know I have this job to do. I can't stop until it's finished.'

'You mean the trail drive to Dodge. That's the end of your job. All right, I'll meet you there.'

He shook his head. 'No point in that either, Roxie.'

'No point!' she echoed. 'Wayne, it is everything! Now we can have all the things we both wanted – and together. Don't you realize half this ranch is mine, maybe all of it.'

'I understand it,' Trevison replied heavily.

'Then why won't you meet me in Dodge?'

Trevison rose and walked slowly across the room to the stone-faced fireplace breaking the wall's center. He rolled himself a cigarette, lit it and flicked the match into the gray ashes. He was a silent, brooding figure standing there in the shadowy room, trouble creasing his brow and deepening the lines around his wide mouth.

'I said this once, Roxie. I'll say it once more and ask you to not force me to do so again. There's nothing for us. Not here, not there, not anywhere. It's all gone and forgotten. It ended there in Dodge and it will never come back again, no matter what the circumstances.'

Roxie listened to his words. She was utterly

still, only her fingers moving as they traced out a seam in the lap of her dark traveling suit. After a long time she said, 'It's Halla Greer, isn't it, Wayne?'

He shrugged. 'If such a thing was possible, yes, I suppose it would be Halla.'

Roxie, 'I see,' in a low voice. 'And you're no man to settle for second best.'

He shook his head. 'There's no such thing, Roxie. You know that. Either it's all or it's nothing.'

'I'm going on to Dodge tomorrow. I'll be there when you arrive with the herd. If you have come to your senses, you'll find me at the hotel. Goodbye, Wayne.'

She whirled abruptly away from him and crossed the room. She paused in the doorway leading into the rest of the house, her fingers resting lightly on the knob. In a kinder voice she said, 'I'll be waiting for you,' and then she was gone.

A week or so later Jay Farr came off the range. He corraled his horse and stomped across the hard pack to where Trevison and Frank Gringras were talking. Roxie had gone on to Dodge City. Troy Washburn had not been found, and he had not seen Halla since the afternoon of the funeral.

'Reckon we're ready to move,' Farr
160

announced. 'Pull away in the mornin' if you say the word.'

'You figure plenty of extra horses? At least five for every rider?'

'Plenty of horses,' Farr replied patiently.

'How about Indian Creek?'

'Water in it all right. Not much, accordin' to Jesse, but enough.'

'Cook and chuck wagon ready to go?'

Farr said, 'Everything's ready to go, Mr. Trevison.'

'We'll pull away at daylight then. Pass the word along.'

Farr said, 'You still figure on takin' that shortcut? Instead of the regular way?'

Trevison said, 'I am. Long as there's water, we can handle the rest.'

'You're the ramrod,' the old puncher said and turned away.

Gringras spoke then. 'Sounds mighty fine. You sure got that herd ready to go in short order.'

'Still a long way to Dodge City,' Trevison reminded him.

'Expect you'll make it,' the banker replied. 'I've got no doubts about that part. However –'

Trevison swung his hard, driving glance at the man, 'However what? Something on your mind?'

Gringras moved his shoulders nervously. 'Nothing, much. Well, I was just wondering about the money end of it. You plan to draw cash or take a draft?'

Trevison's face was humorless. 'You've been talking to Bradford, I see. Well, don't worry about it. You'll get your money. I'll bring it to you and personally lay it in your hand.'

'Of course,' Gringras said quickly. 'I know that. Forget I mentioned it.' He offered his hand.

Trevison accepted it, shaking it briefly. 'See you in a month or so,' he said, and turned to his bunk.

SIXTEEN

The drive started out well.

Triangle W riders had combed the range and every piece of marketable beef had been rounded up. Near twenty-eight hundred head, Farr told Trevison; as they rode to the crest of the knoll beyond the water hole, and watched the herd get under way.

Trevison had called all his riders together and outlined his plan. They would head north for Indian Creek. There they would water the stock and then swing east, keeping slightly north. This should bring them in a short distance below the usual Red River crossing. It would be a hard drive; they could not afford to lose a single head; and the fewer days they were on the trail, the better it would be.

'Anybody back out?'

Farr said, 'One. Ranny called Lillard that came over from Abilene. Said it looked too much hard work to him but I figure he was a bit shy when it come to trouble.'

'Trouble? What trouble?'

'Trouble we'll prob'ly get from raiders. Goin' this route, we're bound to have it.'

Trevison looked closely at the old puncher. Driving the cattle over this new and uncharted trail was the one single thing they had not agreed upon. He said, 'Don't worry, Jay. We'll make it through.'

Farr shook his head. 'I'm hopin' so. We lose this herd the Washburn place is ruint for sure.'

That first day they covered almost twenty miles, bedding the herd down at sunset in a wide, shallow valley. The cook set up camp on a short hill overlooking the swale, and the meal was ready when they had settled the herd. The wrangler strung his rope corral for the horses and turned it over to the night-hawk. The night guards rode off into the darkness and the day crew came in.

The herd was quiet. They had trailed well and the riders were all in good spirits, lying sprawled around the campfire, drinking coffee, smoking, telling their tales and making their jokes. Somewhere off in the night, one of the punchers crooned softly of a girl in San Antone waiting for her cowboy to return; and Wayne Trevison had his thoughts of Halla Greer.

But they were momentary thoughts. He brushed them away with a quick impatience. There was no use in thinking of Halla, of what might have been – for she was now a part of the past. And Roxie. She would be in Dodge City now. Waiting for him, she had said. Maybe Roxie had the right idea after all. Grab what life offered and make the best of it.

The next day was much like the first. Grass was fair and the herd showed little signs of thirst, mostly because it stayed cool and partly cloudy. By the middle of the following morning, however, it was a different matter. The clouds had blown away, and the sun poured down from an empty sky. The steers turned contrary and restless. Trevison was glad they were not long from Indian Creek.

They reached it just after mid-day, halting the main body of stock a short mile back.

164

Trevison and Farr rode on ahead to look the situation over. They decided the best plan was to water the herd in small bunches, then move them onto a higher plateau a few miles further, for the night. This they did, and it was full dark when the job was over.

It was an easy camp. The herd was satisfied, filled with good feed and plenty of water and the going had been smooth.

'Come tomorrow, it won't be no lark like this,' Farr said that night as they rolled into their blankets. 'Country's fair rough from here east.'

Scouting ahead Trevison found the old puncher to be right. The prairie descended into low, broken hills with many rocky arroyos and sharp draws and red fronted bluffs. He had the herd swerved slightly northward to miss the worst of it, but this slowed them down considerably. When darkness caught up they had lost their good average.

Near noon the next day, hot and dusty, they came up hard against a steep-walled slash canyon, which offered no safe crossing for the herd. Trevison and Farr rode along its rough and ragged edge for a long five miles, before they located a break-off sufficiently wide and gentle to allow the cattle to cross over. It was sunset by the time the herd had reached that point. Trevison, taking no chances on a night stampede so close to the canyon, had the crew drive them back a good two miles to bed them down.

They had lost two steers crossing the ravine that next morning, but Trevison considered himself lucky. The crossing was narrow and the animals behaved surprisingly well. There was just that one bad minute when a small bunch broke and ran. That was when the two longhorns were killed, piling up at the bottom with broken necks.

'Some good in that killin' after all,' Farr said when they were again on the move. 'That one old mossyhorn was a looney anyhow. Always tryin' to break and run. Kept the others all fired up half the time.'

It was the same rough, rock strewn country all that day. They made a poor camp, to the bawling of the restless herd, and the night guards were busy. The stock was on the move, almost of their own accord, well before daylight; seeming to sense the smoother prairie land that lay ahead. Their need for water was again making itself felt. But there was little to be done about that. The river was a long day away.

The crew rode in and turned their horses over to the wrangler. Erickson, drawing water from the barrel on the side of the chuck wagon, turned to Trevison.

'Saw riders up ahead today.'

Farr heard that and moved to Trevison's side. He said, 'How many?'

'Four,' the puncher replied. 'Settin' there on top a hill, watchin' us move up.'

'Look like Indians or white men?' Trevison asked.

Erickson shook his head. 'Not Indians. They was all wearin' big hats.'

'An idea who they were?'

Erickson shook his head. 'Too far off for that.'

Trevison turned away, his face knitted into a study. Farr followed him. 'Could be riders driftin' along. Don't have to be raiders.'

Trevison shrugged. 'That's sure, but this is a long way off the main trail for men changing towns. Better double the night guard.'

Farr said, 'Sure,' and wheeled away. He ckecked. 'It occur to you there might be a couple o' people just hopin' you wouldn't get this herd through? Like maybe Troy and Jeff Steeg?'

'Troy's got everything to lose, if I don't.' Trevison said. 'Steeg I could understand trying to stop us but not Troy. We fail to get this beef to market and turn the money over to Gringras at the bank – it's the end of Triangle W.'

167

'You think that means anything to Troy? No matter what kind of man Virgil was, he kept thinkin' about the ranch. Troy's not that way. He thinks about Troy, nothin' and nobody else.'

'Tom was half in each of them,' Trevison said thoughtfully. 'Too bad the two of them couldn't have been one man. Maybe he would have been more like Tom.'

Farr considered this. 'Reckon that's about right.'

Trevison listened to him clomp away in the dark, and then swung to the corral. He picked up his horse and rode off into the night, striking due east. He rode for the better part of four hours, climbing the low hills; throwing his search in all directions for the glow of fire, the sound of a camp – for anything that would reveal the location of the riders Erickson had seen. But if they were still in the country, they kept well hidden. Trevison returned to his own camp, heartened by the thought it was the last they would spend off the main trail.

There were no signs of the mysterious riders on the following day. The herd reached the smooth country and sensing the river, moved fast. Around the late part of the afternoon the broad, silver band of the Red came into view, and the crew let the herd have its head. It broke and ran, stringing out across the grassland like a brown, gray and white flood, not stopping until it had merged with the river; until the cattle was standing belly deep in the water. When they had slaked their thirst, they began to drift for the opposite shore, to collect there in small bunches.

That was when the raiders struck.

They came from the screening border of trees beyond. A dozen riders or more. Trevison, riding near the back of the herd, caught the crackling splatter of their gun shots, and had sporadic glimpses of them through the dust being churned up on the far bank by the cattle. He yelled at Farr a hundred yards away and dug spurs into his horse's flanks.

Several hundred steers were across, on the firm ground of the opposite side of the river. At the first crash of gunfire they veered madly away, running northward parallel to the river. Water sheeted out in arcing, red-tinged spray as Trevison drove recklessly off the bank. The shots had started the main body of the herd to milling, and now they were attempting to wheel in midstream and go back. There was that immediate danger of disaster in the river.

'Keep them coming across!' Trevison yelled to Farr.

The old puncher, driving hard behind

them, ducked his head in understanding, and spun away, boring straight into the wildly struggling longhorns. A rider came off the bank in front of Trevison, following Farr. Trevison reached the far side coming up onto the rocky ground. A large herd of steers was stampeding upriver, a half dozen men in their wake, hazing them with gunshots and shouts.

At that moment Trevison caught sight of the chuck wagon up ahead. The cook had pulled to a stop and was out of the wagon and down on one knee firing at the raiders with a rifle. He buckled suddenly and fell forward as the raiders swept by.

Jesse Shelton rode up, his face dust caked and strained. He said, 'They got Tim,' and fought to keep his nervous, wild-eyed horse still.

Grim faced, Trevison flung a glance at the herd. Farr and the others were getting it under control. He said, 'Let's go after them, Jesse,' and sent his horse plunging ahead. Shelton came close behind. The stampeding steers were now far ahead, almost lost in the lifting pall of dust and rapidly falling darkness.

Another Triangle W rider swung in beside Trevison. Over in the river the main herd was still threshing around in the water.

Several steers were down, being trampled and drowned as other fear-struck animals struggled to reach solid ground. A gun cracked somewhere ahead and Trevison heard the moan of a bullet over his head.

Three of the raiders were cutting away, coming back and firing as they rode. A fourth was bearing straight for the chuck wagon. Trevison snapped a quick shot at the nearest rider. It was a clean miss and this brought a low curse to his lips. He fired again and this time the man jolted in the saddle, clutching at his leg and veered off. Jesse Shelton and the other puncher were off to his left, shooting steadily. The remaining two riders began to swing away.

'Chuck wagon!' Shelton yelled.

Trevison swiveled his attention to that. It was a rising mass of flames, the horses fighting wildly in their harness to escape the fire. Trevison raced toward it. Jesse Shelton said: 'I'll foller them hounds!' and stopped abruptly. A bullet had caught him. He folded silently and tumbled from the saddle.

Trevison drove hard for the chuck wagon, a blazing torch pulled madly in a wide circle by the crazed horses. It capsized suddenly, throwing a dozen smaller torches, from its interior, up and out into the night as bedrolls, groceries and miscellaneous equipment were flung free. The horses broke loose and went screaming away across the prairie.

The two remaining raiders were lining it for the stampeded stock, now out of sight in a band of trees far on ahead. Trevison, furious at the loss of Shelton, of Tim, the cook, as well as the stock, jerked his horse to a halt. Steadying his gun with a crossed forearm, he took deliberate aim and fired. One of the escaping raiders stiffened and fell heavily. His companion ducked lower over his mount's neck and spurred on. Trevison again took careful bead. But his bullet was low. It struck the man's horse instead. It staggered in flight and went to its knees. Trevison fired again, quickly, and missed. The raider, luck favoring him, ran a dozen yards and caught up his fallen buddy's horse, vaulted into the saddle and was again running hard. Trevison threw another shot at him, but by then he was too distant and the darkness made him a difficult target.

The rider who had sided him with Shelton came up, his face flushed with the excitement. 'Jesse's dead. We go after them?'

Trevison shook his head. 'Better go back and help Jay and the boys. Don't want to lose any more stock. I'll see about the cook.'

The cowboy spun away and Trevison rode on to where the cook lay. He was dead, shot through the chest. Trevison walked to where the wagon still glowed in the darkness. Provisions lay scattered about, along with pots and pans, some of it ruined and beyond use, some of it fairly intact. The water barrel was smashed. Blankets and bed rolls were smouldering lumps. Trevison stood silently in the center of it all, anger not yet gone from his tall frame. It had been a neat, well-planned attack. It had caught them when they were least able to defend the herd. And two men were dead. Jesse Shelton and the cook.

He strode back to the buckskin and stepped to the saddle. A mile away he could hear the bawling of the herd, but he did not immediately turn to them. He went, instead, to where the dead raider lay. Perhaps it would be a face he would recognize, and thereby verify a dull suspicion that was glowing within him. He dismounted and rolled the man to his back. Striking a match, he looked closely at the stiff, drawn features. It was a stranger.

Farr rode up to meet him when he returned. The herd was finally across, drifting slowly away from the river. They were tired, nervous and the crew was holding them in a tight circle.

Farr said, 'Lost a man there in the river.

Horse fell and he drowned 'fore we could get him out from under them critters. Lost about seventy head of stock, too.'

Trevison said, 'They got Jesse and the cook.'

Farr swore softly. 'Mighty hard to take. We goin' after them?'

Trevison shook his head. 'Probably the worst thing we could do. They'd sure be back soon as we got out of sight. I think we all better sit tight with the herd until daylight. Then I'll do a little looking around.'

'Reckon you're right. Hate losin' all them steers, though. How many you figure they got?'

'Good three hundred head.'

'How about the chuck wagon? I saw it burnin', seems like.'

'They set it afire. Most of the grub is lost. And the water. Guess we can make out until we reach the next town, but you better name somebody to cook so he can get a meal started. We'll night camp about a mile ahead.'

Farr cut around and disappeared into the darkness. Trevison rode to where Shelton lay. Dismounting, he shouldered the man's body to his saddle and led the horse to the edge of the trees. Here he laid the man down beyond the reach of the herd. He brought

174

up the cook and then the raider and placed them beside the puncher. The cowboy who had drowned in the river was brought in by Erickson.

Later, with Erickson, he set about collecting the food, and other items that were usable. When Farr and the herd moved into the swale for the stop, they had a camp of sorts established. The men were subdued and sobered by the deaths of Shelton and the others. They wordlessly assisted the new cook in getting the fire going, and performed the many chores attendant to getting the meal ready without being asked. When they had finished with their light rations, they exchanged guard duty with the other riders, so they might eat.

They buried the four men there off the trail piling rocks over the graves and marking them with crude crosses. In the flickering torchlight they had lain them side by side, the raider with them, for even a man such as he deserved a decent burial.

The nighthawk had his rope corral up and when Trevison, far from sleep, went there for a mount which he would use in looking over the herd, he found the wrangler standing near Shelton's sorrel pony, rubbing him affectionately along the nose.

'Reckon this old hoss'll miss Jesse,' the

man said as Trevison came up. 'Jesse had
him learned to nuzzle for sugar.' He paused.
'Was you near Jesse when he got his, Mr
Trevison?'

Trevison said, 'Yes. It was quick.'

The wrangler looked off, his gaze on the
faint, distant shine of the river. 'Lot of men
layin' under the ground on this old Trail.
Good ones and bad ones both. You reckon
it'll always be like that? Shootin' and killin'
and raidin' a man's cattle like they done? Why
can't they get some law up here?'

'They'll have it some day, Dobie,' Trevison
said. 'Thing like this can't go on forever.'

'Sure like to lay my sights on the ranny
what shot old Jesse. And Tim, too.'

'The one that got Jesse is dead. We buried
him back there in the trees.'

'But he's dead too late for Jesse. You need a
horse, Mr Trevison? How about takin' Jesse's
sorrel? I think he'd like for you to be ridin'
him out there tonight.'

Trevison nodded and swung to the horse's
back. The saddle was not large enough for
his liking, and he knew the sorrel was tired
– but he would not ride long. Just a short
run to look at the cattle. By then he would
be sleepy. He smiled to the wrangler and
moved off into the darkness. Anyway, why
argue with a sentimental cowboy?

176

They replenished their food stores at a small town in the Indian Territory, obtaining also a wagon that would serve their purpose. The herd moved along at a good average speed, feeding well. Being one of the first drives, the grass was yet in fine condition.

They lost twenty more head near the Canadian River when a crashing thunderstorm struck and set the herd to running. Trevison and Farr kept them stampeding the right direction however, and when the race was over they had gained a few miles despite the loss of steers.

After that, days were much the same, starting early – ending late – with always a sharp lookout for raiders. That particular night, as they made camp a few miles from the North Fork of the Canadian, Farr asked, 'You think we'll run into that stock of ours in Dodge? Doubt if they're far ahead of us.'

Trevison said, 'Don't think it's likely. They'll never go to Dodge. They'll swing wide, missing the town and heading on for Montana or the Dakotas.'

'Not much of a herd to drive that far,' one of the riders commented.

'The steers they get from us are just a part of their herd, if it's one of the usual raider bunch. They get together and hit the trails for a month or so, collecting all the beef they can get, and hiding it somewhere off the main run. Then they blot the brands and put on their own. When they got a fair sized herd, they drive it to a railhead someplace and sell it.'

'Why you figure they won't get to Dodge?'

'Most drives on the trail end there. Less chance of them getting spotted at some other railhead.'

'Sure like to set my eyes on one of them critters with a Triangle W brand on it,' the puncher said. 'Have me some fun makin' the jasper with it explain where he got it.'

'Don't worry,' Farr said pouring himself another cup of coffee, 'we'll never set our peepers on them steers again – and know it. They'll be wearin' somebody else's mark by then.'

They crossed the sluggish Cimarron and were in Kansas, four days out of Dodge City. Trevison did not ride on ahead, as many a trail boss did. For one thing, he still searched for the raiders and the missing steers, making wide forays each night and working far ahead of the herd during the daylight hours, hoping to pick up their trail. But it would seem they had disappeared from the face of the earth. He found no trace of them.

SEVENTEEN

They bedded the herd down about three miles south of town. It was cool and cloudy and it had showered briefly that morning. The cattle were quiet and willing to stop to graze on the sparse prairie. Leaving Jay Farr in charge, Trevison rode into Dodge City.

It was shortly before noon and the streets were teeming with traffic. He traveled the length of Front Street and two others, hauling up finally at the railroad office. Tying up at the rail, he entered the small quarters where a man with sharp eyes, and quick, bird-like movements sat behind a scarred desk. He glanced up at Trevison, smiling.

'What can I do for you, cowboy?'

'Looking for Phillips, the agent.'

'That's me,' the man said heartily. He came out of his chair, surveying Trevison's trail stained shape. 'You the man bringing in that big herd from Texas?'

Trevison said, 'My name's Crewes. I

179

brought in a herd. Whether it's the one you heard about I wouldn't know. I've got them bedded down a little ways below town. Thought maybe you could put me in touch with some buyers.'

'Sure,' Phillips said. He reached into his inside pocket. 'Got a letter here for you.'

Trevison took the note, sealed in a railroad company envelope, and ripped it open. It was a receipt for three hundred and twenty six steers. It was made out to Troy Washburn, who was signing, it noted, for James Crewes.

'Washburn said you'd be along later with the rest of the cattle. I was to hold these in the pens until you arrived.'

Trevison turned the envelope over in his hands. It was addressed to James Crewes – not Trevison. Trevison's mind raced ahead to an understanding. Troy had executed the raid and then repented his actions. And in that there was some sort of victory; Troy, at last had come of age, had accepted his responsibilities and become a man. Too, he had labeled the note for Crewes, not Trevison, indicating he was respecting the big man's desire to remain unknown.

Anger lifted in Trevison then. Maybe Troy was sorry for what he had done, but forgetting was not that easy – nor so simple. Three good men, not to mention the raider, were dead beneath the dust along the trail, all because of him. And that was hard to overlook.

Phillips said, 'Washburn went on. Said he'd see you at the ranch.'

'When was he here?'

'Day before yesterday. What happened anyway? You get separated somehow?'

Trevison said, 'Yes, that's the way of it. Now, where's those buyers? Like to get that herd off my hands before the day's over.'

Phillips lifted a flat-crowned hat from a halltree and moved to the doorway. 'Only one man in town now but prices are good. He'll pay you top.'

They walked to the Dodge House and found the buyer, a man named Gunderson. They had a drink together and then all three, with a tally man, returned to where Farr held the herd. Gunderson spent an hour working through the cattle, checking them critically and when he was satisfied, came back to where Trevison and Farr waited with Phillips.

'Pretty good shape,' he commented. 'Always like these early drives. Beef's good. I'll give fourteen dollars.'

Trevison considered for a moment. 'Make it fifteen and you've got a deal.'

Gunderson thought that out, plucking at the loose skin under his chin. 'Sold,' he said finally. 'Move 'em to the loading pens. My man here will do the tallying – with one of yours, of course.'

Trevison ducked his head at Farr. 'He will look after our end of it.'

Farr swung away to get the herd moving. Gunderson settled himself back into Phillips' buggy. 'How do you want your money?'

'Twenty-five hundred in cash so I can pay off the men. A draft on the rest. Make it payable to Frank Gringras, West Texas State Bank. It's at Canaan.'

Gunderson wrote it all down in a small, folding note book. 'Meet you in Phillips' office, ten o'clock tomorrow morning. So long.'

The buggy sliced away and started for town. Trevison stepped to the saddle and followed Farr, already getting the herd into motion. After it was underway, he rode up beside the old puncher and told him about Troy and the steers waiting in the loading pens. When he was finished, Farr wagged his head.

'Sure took an almighty long time, but I guess that boy's finally growed up.'

'Only one thing wrong with it,' Trevison said.

Farr said, 'Yeh? Now, what's that?'

'There's four men dead back there on the

trail. Troy's growing up came a little late for them.'

The tally man was waiting when they moved the herd in toward the pens. Trevison showed him the receipt for the three hundred odd head Troy had left, and the man took up the count from there. Trevison helped for the better part of the afternoon, and then went on into town after telling Farr to bring the crew to the Dodge House for the night.

The release from the long drive and its weighty responsibilities was beginning to make itself felt, as he rode into a livery barn and stabled his horse. It was difficult to believe the job was almost done; that the endless hours of worry, and tension, and everlasting vigilance against the many dangers were done. It was like coming alive again. Like a condemned man receiving a last minute, unexpected reprieve. That thought sobered him.

The stableman came up, taking the leathers from his hand. Trevison said, 'You the owner here?'

The man said, 'Sure. Name's Jenson. Something I can do for you?'

'Got about fifty head of horses I'd like to sell. They're out near the loading pens. You interested?'

The stableman looked thoughtful. 'Well,'

he said cautiously, 'Might be. Horses not worth much around here. Every trail herd comes up dumps their nags here in Dodge. Keeps prices beat down pretty low.'

Trevison said, 'Take a look at them anyway. Triangle W brand. I'll be at the Dodge House if you want to make me an offer. Name's Crewes.'

Trevison strolled along the street, having his look at old and familiar places, remembering the good things that were in his mind. He registered at the hotel, informing the clerk that his crew of eleven men would arrive later, and to have quarters ready for them.

At the old Long Branch saloon he had a drink and from there went to the barber shop. He waited his turn for a hot bath in the tin tub in the back room. Afterwards he had a shave and a haircut, preserving most of the beard acquired on the trail. He made that one concession to caution. He doubted if anyone in Dodge would recognize him, but he was so near the finish line now he was taking no chances.

He bought himself some new clothes: levis, a couple of shirts, a new pair of boots, underwear and a jumper at Zimmerman's place. He wound up the shopping spree with a steak and potato meal at the BonTon

Café. When Farr and the crew came into Dodge House at full dark, he was sprawled contentedly in one of the deep chairs in the lobby.

'That's for me,' Farr grinned and went to his room.

Trevison advanced the crew money, from the amount he had drawn in Canaan for expenses at the beginning of the drive, advising them to meet him the following day at the railroad office when he would pay off in full. They went their ways, some to follow the same pattern he had just concluded, others to celebrate the end of the trail in typical manner.

The stableman came in soon after that, bringing with him a man he introduced as his partner. Trevison accepted their offer, reserving enough mounts and pack animals for the return trip. Thus it was all done; nothing remained now except the meeting with Gunderson and the payoff. Then it was back to Canaan.

He had considered the possibility of sending the remaining money and draft back with Jay Farr, knowing it would be in safe, honest hands. But he had told Gringras he would finish the job and lay the money in his hands personally. And until that was done, his obligation to Tom Washburn was incomplete.

Farr could do this for him but he would not have it that way.

He walked out into the street. Dodge City was in full night bloom, lights from the stores and saloons bringing all things alive. He started along the dusty way, thinking again of Canaan, of Halla Greer. Like a picture, he could remember the way she looked at him; the deep, mysterious seriousness of her, the cool grayness of her eyes that looked upon him, with such calm reserve and remoteness.

But Halla, however indelibly she was stamped upon him, was not for him. He kept telling himself that knowing it to be utter fact. A door had closed that day Virgil Washburn had died, and Roxie had turned to him for solace. And it was a door he dared not reopen for it could lead to nothing but emptiness.

He thought then of Roxie. She was here in Dodge, waiting for him. Then he thought of Halla Greer – the woman he loved . . . Roxie would have to forget him – he could never go to her.

He stood for a minute, there at the edge of the street, while people pushed by him and the dust hung like a thin, silver fog in the canyon between the buildings. Talk, shouts, laughter and the hammering of pianos floated lightly through the warm night. Somewhere, over near the Long Branch, an exuberant

cowboy emptied his revolver, the shots hollow
and flat.

EIGHTEEN

He rode into Canaan on a bright June day
with the sun streaming out of a cloudless sky.
Jay Farr, and the five men who had elected to
return to the ranch, had cut off back up the
trail and likely now were making themselves
at home in the Washburn bunkhouse. Three
horses stood hipshot in front of the Longhorn
and further along, he noted Noble Greer's
yellow-wheeled buggy at the general store;
the rancher was probably taking on some
supplies. Trevison headed for the bank.

Frank Gringras sat at his desk and the
clerk behind his wire cage thumbed through
a stack of papers as Trevison entered. The
banker came out of his chair hurriedly, a
broad smile wreathing his face.

'Trevison! Sure good to see you! You made
a right fast trip.'

Trevison nodded his greeting. 'A thing I
wanted to get done in a hurry,' he said drily.
He withdrew the letter from his pocket, the
same envelope Troy Washburn had left for

him with the railroad agent. 'Everything's in here. The draft, and what money I had left from the cash after paying off the crew. Look it over and see if it tallies.'

Gringras laid it aside. 'Later be all right? Or are you in a hurry?'

'Figure to ride on tonight if everything's settled up. Appreciate your checking it right now.'

The banker emptied the envelope on his desk. He counted the money and figured for a minute with his pencil. Then he said, 'Right to the penny. Except, you didn't draw your own wages.'

'None necessary,' Trevison answered with a shake of his head.

'But Tom said you were to be paid. Hundred dollars a month. Only right you should take it.'

'Maybe,' Trevison said. 'But I don't need it and I don't want it. I will keep the bay horse I'm riding, if that's all right with you.'

Gringras said, 'Well, if that's the way you want it. The horse is yours, of course.' He paused. 'Troy says he was there in Dodge.'

'Ahead of me,' Trevison said non-committally. 'I didn't see him.'

'Mighty fine thing, way that boy's changed. He'll do all right now. Tom can thank you for that, too.'

Trevison gave him a bitter smile. 'Doubt if it's any of my fault. Everybody grows up someday.'

'I suppose,' Gringras said absently. 'Sorry you want to push on. Country's wide open for good cattle growers. You could do right well around here on a ranch of your own. I expect you could stay on and run the Washburn place, if you took it in mind to.'

'Guess I'm not the settling down kind,' he said and offered his hand. 'Thanks for the help.'

Gringras smiled. 'It's my thanks to you.'

Trevison said, 'So long,' and turned to the doorway.

He stepped outside and walked a half dozen feet into the street, throwing his glance again toward the general store. Greer's buggy was still there, and now Halla sat in the seat while her father loaded a box in the rear. As he looked, Halla turned and saw him standing there. She started, a smile breaking across her lips.

In that same instant Jeff Steeg's coarse voice came reaching across from Longhorn, shattering the quiet.

'Hello, Trevison! Been waitin' around for you!'

Trevison wheeled slowly about, the impact

of the man's tone conveying its message of danger to him.

'Went and done me a mite of checkin' while you was gone. Over in Abilene, at the marshal's office. They got a real nice picture of you there, Trevison.'

So time had finally run out after all. Trevison settled gently in his tracks, squaring himself away. The old coolness sifted through him; the danger-ridden moments of the long trail were once again with him. It turned him grim and nerveless, once more the lone wolf with the instinct to live, to kill to live. He watched Steeg narrowly, seeing him move deeper into the street. He came to a spraddle-legged halt thirty feet away.

'Best thing about that picture, Trevison, was what it said. One thousand dollars reward! Dead or alive!' Steeg's face was a leering, grinning mask.

The street had become a breathless, silent canyon of trapped heat. Behind him Trevison could hear Gringras and his clerk, the scraping of their boots plain as they moved to a window to watch. Halla and her father, he knew without looking, were still there. But nobody else. Only the empty, twisted street.

Trevison said, 'All right, Steeg. It's up to you.'

'That's the way you want it?'

'You'll have to take me.'

From the corner of his eye Trevison saw the figure of Sheriff Bradford come out of his office and halt suddenly. A moment later the man's voice called out: 'Hold up there, Jeff! Wait a minute!'

Steeg laughed, a harsh and grating sound. 'Stand back, Sheriff: He's my pigeon. Worth a thousand dollars in gold to me up in Montana, dead or alive. And he wants it dead!'

'Wait . . .' Bradford's voice sang out again.

Trevison saw the break in Steeg's expression as he went for his gun. His own hand down-flashed. It came up, his gun firing twice. Steeg caught both bullets. He stiffened, fell, dead before he struck the ground.

Trevison remained in that pose, half crouched. He swung slowly to Bradford, eyes dark, glittering slits.

'All right, Sheriff. Let's finish it now. What I said goes for you too. You'll have to take me back!'

Bradford hauled up short. 'Put up that gun, Trevison! That's what I was trying to tell Jeff.'

Trevison was conscious of Gringras coming up from behind, of Bradford's rattle of words. He turned slightly and saw Halla. She was staring at him, her face a mirror of horror, her

191

eyes filled with fear.

'You're not wanted in Montana, Trevison. I did a little checking too, with the sheriff there in Miles City. I wired him about it after I saw that dodger in Abilene. Seems the deputy that testified against you, got himself shot up and when he was dying, confessed they had hung a frame on you.'

Halla was getting down from the buggy. He saw her reach the ground and whirl toward him.

'Happened three or four months ago. You been worrying about your back trail all that time for nothing.'

Trevison heard the words in a maze of confused clamor within his own mind. It was coming hard to him, this realization he was at last a free man, that he no longer need fear the shadows and closed doors, and that which lay around a corner. He opened his arms and Halla came rushing into them. He drew her close.

'Oh, Wayne!' she sobbed. 'I didn't know how much you meant to me until I saw you standing there – standing – facing him with a gun!' She trembled violently.

Trevison pressed her to him, the last vestige of reluctance flowing from him. He said softly, 'Never mind. It's all finished now. Over for good.'

192

'I don't care about anything, about anybody! I'll go with you anywhere, do what you have to do . . .'

She had not heard Bradford's words. She still did not understand what had happened. He felt humble there with her in his arms, hearing her declare her love for him – regardless of who he was – and what lay before him.

He said, 'There's no cause for any of that now. I've been cleared in Miles City. There's no longer any price on my head.'

It took a long moment for the meaning of that to break through her anxiety, to reach her. And then a long sigh escaped her lips. 'Then you can stay. You don't have to go.'

'Not unless you want me to, Halla.'

'Nothing matters,' she said. 'Nothing, as long as we're together.'

From his shoulder he heard Gringras say, 'Come in when you got time and we'll talk about that spread for you. What I said back there in the bank still goes.'

Noble Greer chuckled. 'You're wasting your time, Frank. Looks like Trevison's already got himself a place to look after – mine.'